THE GREEK'S MARRIAGE REVENGE
Clare Connelly

First published 2015

(c) Clare Connelly

Photo Credit: dollarphotoclub.com/Aleksandr Doodko

Contact Clare:

http://www.clareconnelly.co.uk
Blog: http://clarewriteslove.wordpress.com/
Email: Clareconnelly@outlook.com

Follow Clare Connelly on facebook for all the latest.
Join Clare's Newsletter to stay up to date on all the latest CC news.
http://www.clareconnelly.co.uk/subscribe.html

PROLOGUE

Twenty years earlier.

"I'm so hungry," Helena shivered, her frail seven-year-old frame curled over like a conch shell. The rain was lashing in from every direction, but she had the most sheltered spot in the litter-strewn street. Beneath a threadbare awning, her grotty face dry, her matted hair only a little damp; it was the best Alessandro could do.

"I'm going to find you something to eat," Alex swore with more determination than clue. "And one day, Helena, we're going to live like Kings."

Helena's teeth chattered. "I-I-I'm not a boy."

"No," he agreed, looking from one direction to the other. The commuters were still drifting down the cobbled laneway. It was too early. Soon, though, he'd head out to the restaurant precinct and take what he could. Discarded meals, ignored wallets. Anything that would keep his little sister going. It was harder for her. She was so skinny her bones were protruding through her olive skin; he was big and strong, despite the hunger that constantly gnawed at his gut. He'd got used to it. At fourteen, he could rationalise it. He could tell himself it was temporary.

Alessandro Petrides was determined not to let homelessness, poverty or fear control him.

He sat down beside Helena and the dirty street water soaked through his already sodden pants. "You need to think your way out of this. Imagine yourself on a tropical beach. Imagine you're warm and dry and your belly is full of food."

"But I'm so hungry I could die."

"Don't die," Alex responded jokingly, but inside, his heart was breaking. For three years he'd fought for them.

He'd kept them alive, but they weren't really living. What kind of existence was this? "I'd miss you."

"You'd only have one of us to feed though."

How could his sweet little Helena have such a sad understanding of their state in the world? He put an arm around her shoulders. "I'd give my last meal to you, Helena. You know that." He kissed her head. "It's just you and me, okay? We're going to be fine."

"How do you know?"

"Because I'm your brother. It's my job to look after you."

"But ..."

"No buts," he contradicted. "Forever and ever, whatever you need, I will be there for you." He nudged her with his body. "Just promise me you won't quit."

* * *

Twenty years later.

"There is no way your husband is cheating on you, Helena. You are being paranoid."

"I'm not!" The agony in his sister's voice reached him, across the continent to his palatial home on the ragged cliffs of Corfu.

"Of course you are. I know Eric. He is one of my oldest friends. He is a good man."

"Trust you to defend him!"

Alex exhaled a long, slow breath and tried to bring his impatience to order. "If he has slept around, believe me, Helena, I will be the first to condemn his behaviour. But you have no proof."

"I don't need proof."

Alex shook his head ruefully. Beneath him, the moon bathed the cresting waves of the Ionian in a pale milky glow.

"You haven't seen her."

"The nanny?" Alex scoffed. For Eric Sandhurst was hardly the kind of man to sleep around with menials in his employ.

"Yes, the nanny." It was a hiss from between her teeth. "Sophie bloody Henderson. All perfect, blonde, five foot nothing of her."

Alex ran a hand over the back of his neck, dragging his fingers through the dark hair that curled a little at his nape. "Then your solution is simple. If you truly believe this to be true, fire her."

"I tried! Eric won't let me!" Her voice was becoming higher in pitch; her tone obviously desperate.

Alex's dark eyes, almost as dark and shimmering as the night sky beyond him, were focussed on a trawler in the distance. The nets were lowering, and the boat was lurching in the movements of the current.

"It is a domestic decision. You do not need to listen to him. He is barely around to object, I should have thought."

"That might have been the case before we hired her, but now? He's like a love-sick puppy. He follows her to the park with the children. He makes sure he is home for story time. They curl in the bed together and read to the boys. Please, Alessandro, you know I would not trouble you with this if I were not truly afraid for my marriage."

Alex's fingers curled more tightly around his phone. His sister had always held a flare for the dramatic. It was entirely possible that she was imbuing perfectly innocent scenarios with a degree of fault that didn't belong. "Why do you not partake in these events too?"

"You are blaming me for his infidelity."

"Alleged infidelity," Alex corrected automatically. "And of course I am not. I am simply reminding you that it is your house. They are your children. He is your husband. You are not forbidden from spending time with them."

"I'm an outsider." She sobbed quietly, but Alex heard it, and it tore his heart in two. His sister was grieving, regardless of what the facts might be. "The way he looks at her ... I know he loves her. Because it is how he once looked at me."

A small kernel of worry lodged in Alex's gut. He knew that his sister's marriage had been troubled. The difficulties they'd experienced conceiving, coupled with several miscarriages and finally, children who were boisterous and exhausting at times, had strained them.

"I think you must fire her."

"Eric may leave me."

"Of course he won't leave you." Apart from anything, Alex's old friend was ambitious as hell. His desire to one day run for mayor of London would smother any divorce notions. Even if he no longer loved Helena? Is that what Alex wanted? For his only sister, a woman he had virtually raised, to be in a marriage with a man who didn't love her?

"Perhaps you and he should get away for a time. Come here, to Greece, where I can talk with him."

"No!" Her voice shook. "I already suggested a vacation. He told me he has too much work on."

Alex's kernel of doubt was gaining in size and weight. He didn't want to think the worst of his friend. And yet, his sister was clearly not going to be placated.

"*Paidi mou,* do not make yourself uneasy. I will come to you."

"And will you end it, Alex?"

His laugh was a harsh sound in the night. "Believe me, if there is something going on, I will bring an end to it."

CHAPTER ONE

"Ian! John! Come here now!"

"We're hiding!" The sweet little voice, unmistakably Ian with it's huskier tone, emerged from beneath the sofa. Sophie made a show of lifting the cushions on an opposite dais before moving towards the piano. She sat on the stool with a melodramatic sigh and pretended not to see the chubby, tanned fingers splayed across the floor.

"I do hope I haven't lost those twins. Their mummy and daddy would be so cross with me."

A giggle erupted – she couldn't have picked which twin it belonged to, for their laughs were identical. Matching little peals of amusement that always brought an answering grin to her own face.

"Then again, I suppose I could dress their teddies up in the boys' clothes. Perhaps that would fool them. I would, of course, need to take the teddies to the park. And feed them their marmite toast." Another giggle.

She walked across the room and picked up one of the teddies. It was threadbare in places, from having been hugged so tight.

"What do you think, Mr Teddy? Would you be Ian? Or John?" She tapped his little nose and then crouched down onto her knees. "What's that Mr Teddy? You see them? Where?" She pushed the bear under the sofa and moved his head up and down. The giggles were loud now, loud enough to reach the three people assembled in the corridor. Helena, her face pale, looked nervously towards the lounge area.

Alex followed her gaze. His sister was hardly herself. Where once she had smiled easily, her face was now pinched. "Where are my nephews? I am anxious to see them."

Eric apparently didn't perceive a hint of tension. Nor did he question the unexpected arrival of his brother-in-law.

That a man as powerful as Alessandros Petrides should decide on a whim to visit was not unusual. Alex had always marched to the beat of his own drum, and done very much as he wished, when he wished it. Eric was simply pleased to see the man he cared so much for. He put an arm forward, indicating that Alex should move into the lounge area.

When they arrived at the door, Sophie was lying on her stomach, half under the sofa. What Alex could see earned a flicker of interest. Her waist was narrow, and her shirt had lifted to expose several inches of honey-coloured skin. She wore pale jeans that showed off her slender, curved legs and rounded rear. Her feet were bare.

"Oh, Mr Teddy. How right you were. You are a genius, and so beautifully furry too. What did we do before we found you?" Giggles emerged from beneath the furniture; two boys and one woman's. Her accent was Australian, her tone pleasingly soft.

"Now, we have a serious mission this evening, boys."

"What? What-iddit?" The voice of John emerged, slightly blurred by laughter.

"Ah. You'll have to come out with me if you want to know that. Are you ready? Shall we fly out together?"

"Fly? We can't fly."

"Of course you can. So long as we hold hands, we can do anything."

"No, that's not true." Ian was always more serious than his brother; he was a thinker, intent on knowing how things worked. "Little boys can't fly."

"Well, ordinarily not, no." She leaned closer, and in the darkness beneath the sofa, she saw both boys clamour closer, their eyes shining. "But have I ever told you about Peter Pan and the lost boys?"

They shook their heads in unison. "Goodness me. What an omission. Perhaps that is the book we shall read next." She held hands with both boys. "Now, I don't personally have any fairy dust with me right now, but we will learn, from the book, where I can get some."

"Fairy dust?" Ian was sceptical, and it brought a small smile to Sophie's lips.

"Or so they say." She shifted her head so that she could see John; it was no mean feat in the small space she occupied.

"I want to read the book!" It was John. Always enthusiastic and ready for adventure. In many ways, he was a kindred spirit of the lovable Peter Pan.

"Well, let me see if I can remember what we need to say. *Second star to the right, and straight on 'til morning.*"

The boys did their best to repeat it, and then Sophie began to slide backwards, with the boys inching along behind her. Their hiding was forgotten now; one adventure completely swamped by the promise of another.

Sophie stood, and for the first time, became aware that there were other people in the room.

Alex was, momentarily, transfixed.

Helena had not exaggerated this woman's charms. In fact, Helena, as a woman, perhaps didn't even completely comprehend the sensual promise that was offered in every inch of this petite, curvaceous woman. From her shimmering blonde hair that was scraped carelessly into a pony tail, to the wide-set, clear blue eyes and dainty nose with a little ski jump tip, to the lips that were full and pink, to a body that men would go to war for and skin that was soft and golden, the nanny was undeniably gorgeous.

"We've been hiding," she said unnecessarily, her manner instantly guarded compared to how she'd been with the boys.

Her eyes skimmed past Eric and landed on Helena. Her smile seemed forced. Then, she looked at Alex, and her blue eyes flew wide as she stared at him. His lips curled in sardonic amusement. Her appraisal was brazen. She made no efforts to disguise her interest, running her clear gaze from his thick black hair to his broad shoulders, and lower still, down the length of his muscular frame. He saw the way her delicate neck bunched as she swallowed, and he liked it.

He enjoyed her confusion, for it was an obvious sign that she was affected by him.

"*Thios*!" John launched himself forward and wrapped his arms around his uncle's legs. Ian followed suit, more tentative but obviously loaded with affection. And the spell was broken. She took a step back to visibly separate herself from him, and the feelings that were coursing through her.

"Soph, this is my brother-in-law Alessandros Petrides." Alex noticed the shortened version of her name with a jolt of disapproval. He smothered his scowl.

Sophie had heard of him, of course. Who hadn't? The self-made billionaire who was as renowned for his successes in the boardroom as the bedroom.

Only Sophie hadn't made the connection between Helena and this man. Now that she looked at them, she could see a similarity in their features, and certainly in their bearing. But how could she have guessed that Helena was related to a man such as this? Her mouth was dry, her throat suddenly thick and constricted.

"Hello." A tiny noise, husky and sultry, Alex felt yet another pull of curiosity.

He extended a hand, and told himself he was practicing a convention rather than seeking an excuse to touch her. Sophie acted on autopilot, sliding her own small hand into his. The gesture of greeting sparked an unwelcome flash of desire in his blood stream. She was warm and soft. Her eyes flashed with confusion and she quickly pulled her hand back, eyeing her employers with a guilty flush.

"Pleased to meet you," she husked hurriedly. "Now, if you'll excuse us, the boys and I have an adventure ..."

He cut her off easily, and enjoyed the way pink colour spread into her cheeks. "I should like to spend time with my nephews."

"Oh, of course." Sophie blinked. It was obvious that this thought had never occurred to her. For some reason, she hadn't pictured Alessandros as the kind of man who would enjoy spending time with children.

"Eric, why do you not take my sister out for the evening. Sophie and I will manage the children."

Eric hesitated for a fraction of a second, and then nodded. "Yes, a good idea. Helena? Can you get ready quickly?"

Helena was visibly pleased. Her face lifted in relief as she nodded. "Of course!"

And she did. No longer than ten minutes later, Helena and Eric pulled the door shut behind them, leaving Alex, Sophie and two excitable young children in the hallway.

"What have you brought for us, *thios*?"

Alex's laugh sent darts of emotion down Sophie's back. "John," she employed a serious tone despite her amusement. "We don't ask for gifts. It is bad mannered."

"Oh." A petulant lower lip jutted out. "But *Thios* Alex always brings us things."

She crouched down and took both of his hands in hers, ignoring the way Alex's gaze made the hairs on the back of her neck stand on end. "Isn't it enough of a gift that he's come to see you?" She smiled at Ian, softening her admonishment with a kind expression. "Come. We don't want your uncle to think you care only for what gifts he might carry."

Alex was, grudgingly, impressed by the lesson she was bestowing. Though he and Helena had grown up with nothing, those years were far behind them. It had been a long time since Helena had enjoyed great personal wealth, and he had silently feared that his nephews were being raised with a great appreciation for possessions.

"Now, why don't you take your uncle upstairs while I fix your tea."

"Tea is what they call dinner in 'Strarlia." Ian explained, his expression serious.

Sophie stood and the self-consciousness returned when she looked at Alex. "Their rooms are the second and third to the right," she said, nodding at the stairs.

Alex's smile didn't reach his eyes. No, his eyes were softly calculating. "Boys," he spoke without removing his gaze from her face. "Go to your rooms. I will be along in a moment."

Ian moved quickly but John was preparing to mount a complaint. "Now, John." Alex murmured, his eyes dropping to her full lips, and then lower still, to the skin at her décolletage.

Sophie swallowed nervously. "You don't need to help me."

"No," he agreed with a firmness to his voice. "But I would like to."

Two pink spots appeared in Sophie's cheeks. It was on the tip of her tongue to object but she thought better of it at the last minute. This was her employer's brother, and also a very powerful man. He was a guest in the house, and she was staff. It was certainly not her place to tell him to leave her alone.

"Fine," she muttered, her smile tight. "The kitchen's…"

"It is not necessary for you to tell me where things are in the house. I have been here before."

Her flush deepened. "Not since I've worked here."

"And how long is that?"

Sophie lifted her eyes to his face and then looked away again instantly. "Nine months."

A long time. Almost a year. "You are very young."

"I'm twenty four," she bristled defensively.

"I am surprised my sister hired a nanny with such little experience."

His tone rankled. "I beg your pardon, you have no idea what my experience is."

"At twenty four, it can not be vast," he pointed out with a sardonic lift of his brow.

"If you say so." It was a curtly dismissive rejoinder that surprised them both. To cover her embarrassment, Sophie lifted a frying pan onto the stove and lit the ignition, then added some oil to it. She'd diced the chicken earlier and she pulled it from the fridge now, adding it to the oil with a sizzle.

Alex didn't take up one of the seats across the kitchen, but instead propped his hip against the island bench. He was too close. Too big, too intimidating and far too unnerving. "What is your experience?"

Sophie lifted a spoon from the frying pan and shifted the chicken around. "Why do I feel like I'm being interviewed?"

"My nephews are of great value to me. It is natural that I would take an interest in their caregiver."

"Their parents are their caregivers," she clarified. "And they also take a great interest in me."

Yes, he thought with a cynical lift of his lips. How much interest though?

"You've worked privately as a nanny?"

"Yes." Her cheeks flushed. "I worked for two years for a family in Sydney before deciding to come to London." It was a slight fudging of the facts, but this man hardly needed to know the ins and outs of that emotionally stressful time in her life.

"And this was your first post in England?"

"No." She shook her head. "For two months I travelled with the Prime Minister's family. He had various commitments abroad and I was hired in addition to their usual staff. When they returned, he made certain to help me find a good placement."

"Hence you came to work for Helena."

"And Eric, yes." Her smile was indulgent. "It was actually Eric who hired me. He knows the prime minister, and when he emailed Eric, the response was instant. Helena was ..." She lowered her eyes, biting back the words she'd been about to say. Whether that was from loyalty to his sister or out of guilt at backstabbing her to him, Alex couldn't have said for sure.

"Helena was?" He prompted with the appearance of curiosity.

"Helena had her hands full. The boys are very high-octane, as you know. It's not unusual for four year olds, especially boys, but the fact they're twins – they egg one another on."

"And my sister is not maternal?" He queried, voicing his own private feelings in the form of a question.

"Of course she is!" Sophie contradicted, genuine surprise in her eyes. "She's a lovely mother, and the boys adore her. One doesn't need to enjoy going to the park and playing chase and reading stories to be maternal."

"Or hiding under the sofa?" He prompted, reaching forward and pulling a piece of dust from her hair. She watched as he eyed it and then dropped it to the floor.

"Exactly. I enjoy that stuff. I love playing with the boys."

"It is your job to enjoy it."

"It is my job *because* I enjoy it," she corrected. "I wouldn't do this if I didn't."

"How long will you stay?"

She shrugged. "I haven't made up my mind yet." And besides the fact she hardly knew this man, she found herself speaking with honest uncertainty. "One of the hardest things about my job is leaving the children. In order to do this properly, you have to fall in love with them."

"With only the children?" He prompted, thinking of his brother in law and the suddenly very strong likelihood that he'd formed a crush on this stunning young Australian.

"Well, with the family." She shrugged; her shoulders were slender and vulnerable somehow. "I love them, but I'll leave them at some point. And miss them all like crazy." She flicked a smile at him.

His expression was difficult to interpret. He was someone who kept his feelings perfectly concealed.

"Eric works long hours."

"He's making an effort to curtail that." Another guilty flush. "It's better for the children that he be around more."

"Is it? Why?"

Sophie sighed. "It just is. I see this time and time again. Many families who employ nannies have one parent – or both – who is frequently out of the home. I know that's the demands of jobs, but for the small time when children are young, they benefit enormously from having parents who are present."

"I see," he prompted silkily. If she knew him better, she might have detected the dark note to his voice. But she did not. At that stage, Sophie took Alessandros Petrides at face value.

"Yes. As I explained to Eric, he is well-thought of enough to shape his career around his family for a time."

"And Eric listened to this?" Alex said, disbelief rich in his chest.

"Yes. Well," she laughed. "He's trying. He's a workaholic, you know, but he makes a point of reading to the kids a couple of nights a week, even if he then has to go back to the office."

"And my sister?"

Sophie's shoulders squared defensively. But what was she defending? Her right to be alone with Eric? Or his sister? "What about her?"

"She doesn't join you?"

"Helena spends more time with the children than Eric. She doesn't need to make such a point to carve out special blocks of time." She turned away from him and stirred the chicken again, then added some greens to the same pan.

"I presume you had references? Or did Eric hire you on the spot?"

"I told you," she couldn't flatten the offended sound from her words, "I was recommended personally by the Prime Minister. Prior to taking the role within his family, I was thoroughly background checked." She turned around to face him again, holding the spoon in front of her like a shield. "Why are you asking me these questions? Have I done something to offend you?"

Alex's smile was pure, sexy amusement "Not yet," he shrugged cryptically.

Sophie stared at him in confusion. "The twins will be waiting for you."

"Yes," he agreed, then continued as though she hadn't spoken. "And what do you do, Sophie, when you are not minding my nephews and defending my sister?"

She shrugged, then removed the pan from the heat. "I exist in a state of stasis." She blinked her long lashes at him in an obvious gesture of sarcasm, and then shook her head. "I'm sorry. I don't mean to be rude. But you were ..."

"Being rude first?" He finished the sentence for her, and she broke out in a genuine smile.

"Yeah. Something like that." She tipped the stir-fry into a pair of Thomas the Tank Engine bowls.

She was bewitchingly charming. Was it possible Eric had fallen under her spell? Could he have thrown caution to the wind and engaged in the kind of affair that would break Helena's heart? Not only was it possible, Alex was becoming increasingly convinced that it was highly likely. Despite Eric's political aspirations, Alex suspected Sophie was just the kind of woman who could make him forget everything he owed to himself and his wife.

"Would you please go and get the boys?"

He was still for a moment, lost in thought, and then he nodded, moving from the kitchen. It gave Sophie an opportunity to study him surreptitiously, as he cut across the expansive lounge area and headed to the stairs. He moved with an almost predatory grace. He was silent and stealthy, and yet even then, simply strolling across the ground floor of this Kensington townhouse, he moved with a barely concealed power and strength that made her heart race.

"Get a grip!" Sophie whispered. The incantation cheered her, as it always did. Those three words had been uttered by their mother, *ad infinitum*, whenever she'd needed to call on inner strength. As a result, all three

Henderson sisters used the same phrase whenever they needed to shake themselves out of an annoying mindset.

It served as a reminder to find calm, and also as a talisman of their mother. In the five years since losing her, Sophie wasn't sure a day had passed in which she hadn't thought of Meredith Henderson.

"Are these what you were looking for?" Alex appeared with two boys at his heels, and grouped together like that, Sophie couldn't help but gasp.

Her young charges were so like their uncle! Perhaps that explained why one look at Alex had filled her with a cumbersome sense of familiarity? It wasn't a physical thing, so much as that he reminded her of the children she'd come to love dearly. For he was indeed the grown-up version of these two beautiful little beings. Six eyes, dark and almond shaped, stared at her, their similarities now impossible to miss.

"Sit up, darlings. I've made your favourite."

"Oh, goody yum." John scampered into his seat and Ian followed suit, slightly less enthusiastic in his appraisal of the meal that they regularly requested.

"And if you are very good, and make sure you eat all that yummy kale, there'll be a lolly after dinner."

"Bribing the children with sweets?" Alex queried *sotto voce*.

Sophie grinned and nodded, her heart thrilling at the idea of his disapproval – though she couldn't have said why.

"They're just vitamin lollies, *Thios*," Ian countered. Though he was little, he didn't miss a thing.

"I see."

Sophie sat across from the boys, and indicated with a wave of her hand that Alex was welcome to join them.

His presence made the large space feel constrained somehow. Or perhaps that was just the way his leg brushed against hers beneath the table. She jerked away, not caring that it was an unmistakable gesture of innocence.

She fixed the children with an assessing gaze and then leaned forward. "Fork, darling one." She turned to Alex, ignoring the way her heart began to palpitate in her chest. "John loves to use his fingers. We're working on it, aren't we?"

Alex found it difficult to fault Sophie's credentials as a nanny, at least. She was attentive, affectionate, kind, patient and thorough, not letting either boy leave the table until both had finished their meals, and urging a form of conversation between the two without being overbearing. Though Alessandros had very little experience with children, he had eaten in enough restaurants and witnessed the appalling behaviour of this generation to be impressed. Though he preferred to give his sister some of the credit, he wasn't sure that was deserved.

More seamless supervising as the boys were washed, their teeth were cleaned and they were wrangled into bed.

"But daddy was going to read to us!" Ian said darkly, his eyes moist from unshed tears.

"I know, darling, but daddy and mummy are out discussing grown up things." Alex studied her from the door. Her voice quivered a little, but she didn't otherwise betray any emotional response to the fact that Eric and Helena were enjoying a romantic evening.

Was that because she didn't feel anything? Or because she was so assured of her place in Eric's affections that she didn't care?

Helena's notion had been so easily dismissed before he'd met her. But now?

Coldness gripped his heart. How could Eric live under the same roof as this woman and not notice her numerous charms?

As he watched, Sophie's face lifted towards the door and her eyes lanced his. His stomach clenched with desire, hot and undeniable.

He was used to the effect he had on women, but it was unusual for a woman to stir those same feelings of powerless attraction in him. In fact, he prided himself on his ability to remain detached from almost any situation.

Helena was, of course, an example. Seven years his junior, he loved her almost as a daughter, rather than a sister. She had always been young for her age, and he bore boundless maturity brought on by the responsibilities that had dogged him almost from birth.

He listened as she read to the boys, her voice mesmerising and intoxicating in equal measure. The story was one he hadn't heard; then again, why would he have? Even as children, no one had whispered sweet stories to them as they fell asleep. And as a grown man, he had little time or interest in books.

John was asleep before she'd finished, and Ian was not long behind.

Sophie finished the story though, and then gently closed the pages and stood. She kissed first Ian, and then John, before settling their sheets over their little shoulders.

He intentionally waited in the doorway for her, so that she'd have to brush past him. He didn't know if she was involved with his brother in law, though he suspected it was highly likely.

The only thing he knew for certain was that he wanted Sophie all to himself. For a while at least.

CHAPTER TWO

"She was crying again, Eric." Sophie kept her voice low, and her head bent towards her employer.

"Where?" He was tired. So tired of worrying about his wife, and trying to make her happy and well.

"In the laundry. Early this morning. Before I went for my walk."

"She didn't come to bed last night."

Sophie bit down on her lower lip. The propriety of speaking to Eric about his wife had bothered her at first. But within only a few days of joining the household, Sophie had come to realise that Helena was struggling with the pressures of motherhood and her high profile as Eric's wife. She had been hesitant, at first, to jump to any conclusions, but another few days into her tenure had convinced her that something was badly wrong.

Helena was depressed. She needed to meet with a professional and get proper support.

Only Eric didn't seem to share Sophie's worries. Or, if he did, he was determined to ignore them.

"How was she at dinner?" Sophie blushed at the question, which could have been seen as prying. But not by Eric. He understood. Sophie was worried about Helena, and especially about the boys. He'd come to count on her counsel in the last few months.

"Quiet." He shrugged. "But she is always quiet lately."

"Maybe you should go away for a while, like she suggested," Sophie pushed, lifting a hand comfortingly to his shoulder.

"You're the one who told me how important my place in the boys' life is. I don't want to leave them."

"They could go with you. I could come."

"No."

"Why not?"

"It doesn't solve anything. That's a temporary fix. Whatever is going on with Helena, she needs to right it."

Sophie compressed her lips. "I don't know if it's that easy."

"She has two children. Two children we spent five years trying to bring into being, and who love her and need her. I don't give a shit if it isn't easy. She must do it. There is an imperative on her to meet their needs."

Across the room, Alex couldn't hear what they were saying. Their pose was unmistakably intimate, with their faces close and her arm on his shoulder. They weren't even trying to hide it!

Alex's temper, under a tight reign for two days, began to fray as he realised with a grim frown, that his sister had been right. This beautiful ingénue had come into his sister's life and was now attempting to usurp her place in it.

He was sure of it.

"Be patient. She will find her way." A feint noise caught Sophie's attention and she looked in its direction, straight into the hard, sardonic eyes of Alessandros Petrides. A shiver flexed down her spine. She looked away again quickly. "You have Alessandros here now. Have you spoken to him? Maybe he'd have an idea ..."

"No." Eric's scowl formed a perfect line between his brows. He followed her gaze and shifted into a polite smile. "Listen, Soph. Alex is a ... top chap. But when it comes to Helena, he's controlling as hell. If he thinks she's not happy, he's just likely to put her on a Petrides jet to Greece."

"Surely not," Sophie countered, her eyes drifting back to Alex's face. He was fuming about something; that much was obvious even to Sophie, who knew very little of the Greek billionaire beyond what the press had publicised over the years. "She's your wife ..."

"But she's also his sister, and Alex will always trump me in Helena's mind." He let out a peevish sigh. "He's the quintessential control freak. It's better not to involve him or I'll lose my wife for good."

She laughed despite herself. "And here I thought you were far too staid for melodrama."

He lifted his eyes heavenward. "It might sound melodramatic, but believe me, it's no exaggeration. Alex doesn't believe in second chances."

"Second chances?"

"He gave me a chance when he agreed to our marriage. He was against it at first. Though I doubt he'd have liked any man who married Helena. But he trusted me. And he made it obvious that he was willing to give me one chance to make her happy. If he knows she's miserable, he'll do whatever he can to end it."

"Eric," she shook her head, her eyes so blue there were like denim in the dusk light that filtered in through the bay windows. "You're being ridiculous. Helena is a grown woman. Her life has nothing to do with Alex."

"You mightn't think so, but trust me, he'll make this his business and he'll take over." He shrugged, but his expression was tired. "Listen, we'll stick to the plan. You keep a firm eye on the children, and I'll slowly find a way to get through to her. But *please* keep it between us. Alex being here is a complication I hadn't anticipated."

Eric's eyes moved beyond Sophie. Alex had stopped reclining indolently on the far side of the room and was prowling towards them. A hint of determination sparked in his expression.

Though Sophie and Eric couldn't have known it, a plan, so perfect for its precision and cruelty, had come to Alex, fully formed.

"Sophie." His accent was thick, his voice as seductive as ever. "The children are in bed. You are free for the night, are you not?"

"What?" She blinked, her eyes enormous as she lifted them to his face. He was bewilderingly handsome, particularly dressed as he was now, in a pale shirt that showed off his caramel skin.

He followed the direction of her gaze and rewarded her with a sensual smile, loaded with promise. *I understand*, it said. *I want that too.* "I would like to take you out."

She shook her head, confused and uncertain. "You would like to … take me out?"

Eric looked from one to the other and decided it was his place to save his employee from the overpowering Alessandros Petrides. "Sophie usually goes to bed early, because the twins still stir overnight."

"You don't give her even a night off?" Alex's tone held a note of warning, and Eric didn't miss it. His brows beetled as he studied his friend.

"She's never asked for one," Eric demurred, shrugging his shoulders as though it didn't matter to him.

"Then let this be the first time."

"I'm fine," Sophie interrupted, finally remembering that she had a voice and a say in matters.

His eyes were black and loaded with speculation when he turned to her. "But you do not yet know what I wish to show you."

His intention was set. She would become his. And her mind would become so full of him, and her body would crave only his, so that any thoughts of Eric would flock completely from her mind.

And if he was wrong? If Helena were wrong? And there was an innocent explanation for her apparent closeness to Eric?

He discounted it almost instantly. Oh, of course there was a small possibility. But Alessandros had lived and died by swift decisions, and that attitude had rarely failed him.

Unfortunately for Sophie, Alessandros was not a man who had been born with a proverbial silver spoon. He'd grown up tough, fighting for everything he had in life, and it had turned him into someone who fought dirty, and with any tools at his disposal, if the ends justified the means.

What would he not do for the sister he had raised? Seducing this woman was hardly unpalatable to Alex but he understood it was morally questionable. Only his loyalty to Helena hardened his resolve. He would have Sophie. And sooner rather than later.

Sophie opened her mouth to object but no words came out. She was momentarily mute. This was a man unlike any she'd ever met. He was handsome as sin, gorgeous, in fact, and she was filled with a drowning sense of powerlessness that was foreign to her.

Alex's gaze moved from her eyes to her mouth, and then he angled his face toward his friend. "Good evening, Eric." He put a hand in Sophie's back, and before she could find her voice, or her mind, he ushered her towards the front door.

It was only when they'd reached the pavement outside the elegant townhouse that Sophie stopped walking and stared up at him. "Alessandros ..."

"Alex, please," his voice was barely a breath. A husk of sound that curled around her body and soul.

"Alex, what are we doing?"

His expression was droll, and he easily made her feel like a complete wowser.

"We are walking. Or, at least, we were, until you stopped and said, *Alessandros*." His imitation of her voice sent shivers down her spine. Was that really how she spoke? So husky and intimate?

She turned away from him, embarrassment making her skin crawl. "But why?"

Alex's fingers on her back began to run up and down her spine, sending answering darts of awareness shooting through her whole body. "Sophie, are you going to lie to me?"

"To lie to you?" She repeated softly, lifting a hand to her throat and toying with the necklace she always wore.

"Mmm," he urged her forward and she fell into step beside him. "You are going to lie and pretend you don't want to be here with me?"

"I ..." She was anguished. Had she been so obvious?

"Are you going to lie and say you have not been thinking about me and wondering? Are you going to say you do not feel this same tug of attraction that warms my body when you are near?"

He was being direct. So direct. And with good purpose. He could not afford to delay. Not when his sister's marriage was likely at stake.

He turned the corner and she followed. It was a beautiful, private square lined with elegant Georgian houses. One in the corner had darkly tinted windows and geraniums in the window boxes.

"Well?" His voice was almost a growl.

"Well," she shaped her mouth around the same word, her eyes lifting to his. It was as though she had been singed. There was something so powerfully, ferociously hot in his look, and Sophie wasn't sure she was equal to it.

"You are not going to lie to me after all?"

Sophie was lurching uncertainly. She had limited experience with the opposite sex, and absolutely zero clue with a man like Alex. "I ... don't know what you want me to say."

His laugh was a soft, teasing sound. He ran a thumb over her lower lip, and his eyes chased after it. His body was close to hers. So close she could feel his warmth and smell his intoxicating fragrance.

"I hardly know you," she whispered desperately.

"So?" He dropped his hand to the collar of her shirt and traced the stitching. When his fingers moved close to the dip of her breasts, she drew in a shuddering breath.

"Alessandros." *Step back!* She needed to put some distance between them. Only her hips swayed forward and her eyes fluttered closed.

They were long lashes, dark and curled. Alex stared at her face, and felt a swift jab of compunction for her youth. But this woman could not continue in his sister's home if she harboured feelings for Eric. It was unacceptable.

And it was Alex's job, as had been divined by birth and circumstance, to make sure Helena was kept from harm.

"I will not kiss you here, *agape mou*, for I do not trust that I can control myself to stop."

Sophie's heart turned over in her chest. How she wanted him to kiss her! The very idea was terrifying, and sobering. She could not get involved with a man such as this. Oh, for so many reasons, it would be wrong, wrong, wrong. He was her boss's brother! And a well known womaniser to boot. It would muddy the waters terribly if she allowed herself this indulgence.

But what an indulgence it would be.

She almost groaned when she imagined what it would be like to be kissed by him. For he was strong and confident and most definitely knew how to please a woman.

"That's probably a good idea," she said, relief in her voice that he, at least, was going to be strong enough for both of them.

"Oh, I'm going to kiss you."

Her eyes flared and her stomach rolled.

"Not here though." He put his hand around her shoulders and pulled her gently with him. His walk was faster now, and she had to stride quickly to keep up. It was not far to go though; he paused just outside the house at the corner.

"This is yours?" She asked in surprise.

He nodded. "I bought it when they married."

"To be close to Helena?" She guessed, remembering Eric's assessment that Alex was a meddlesome, overbearing brother.

"Of course to be close to her. And to give her somewhere to stay if it didn't work out."

Sophie slanted a curious gaze up at him, but he was pushing the door inwards.

"Surely Helena doesn't need you to fight her battles for her." The last few words of her statement were lost in the crush of his mouth to hers. He pushed her back against the front door and held her there with his lips alone. His tongue was demanding and Sophie felt her knees going weak with a deluging surge of need. Her insides were slick with heat. She moaned deeply in her throat and lifted her hands to his chest.

He was just as firm to touch as she had known he would be. Firm, strong and warm. Up close he smelled of spice and summer. He was electrifying.

"Alex," it was a passionate cry into his mouth but he didn't release her. Instead, he brought his hands to her back and curled them possessively inside the waistband of her jeans, to cup her naked rear. Sophie hadn't been touched so intimately in a long time, if ever. Her one and only boyfriend had been a spectacularly unimpressive Rohin Smith, from the same little Margaret River school she'd gone to. They'd fumbled around a few times and that had culminated in a very brief coming together, followed by another attempt a week later.

Beyond that, Sophie was an absolute novice.

"Alex!" She pulled her mouth away with effort, and dipped her head forward. She was panting, not from exertion but from the sheer strength of her desire.

The slight darkening along his chiselled cheekbones showed that he was not immune from the power of their kiss.

Sophie tried again. "Alex, I can't get involved with you."

"Can't you?" He murmured, lifting her shirt up to her neck. With a look of frustration, Sophie reached her fingertips to the sky, so that he could remove it completely. Her bra was a sensible, plain cotton piece; certainly not the lace and silk lingerie he was used to on his women, and yet he found it totally alluring.

"What were you saying?" He murmured deeply, as he bent one scrap of fabric aside to reveal a perfect, pert breast.

Sophie gasped as his fingers ran over her nipple possessively. "That you're related to my employers. And that I hardly know you. I can't do this with you."

Alex took her nipple in his mouth and rolled it with his tongue, before pressing his teeth against it lightly. Just enough to sear a sharp wave of painful longing through her. "Do you want me to stop?"

Sophie was hot and cold; pins and needles were in her body and soul.

And Alex understood. He knew the effect he was having on her. He knelt before her and undid her jeans, but he only slid them down to her knees, so that she was virtually imprisoned against the door. He quickly brought his mouth back to her breast, and his fingers he drifted lower, to her most intimate core.

"Do you want me to stop?"

Sophie felt a shudder of delirium as he moved one long finger inside her silky, wet centre.

"Alex?"

"So-phie," he teased, his accent thicker than normal as he transferred his mouth to her other breast. He tasted her through the fabric of her bra, and Sophie cried out impatiently.

"Please," she whimpered, her fingers digging sharply into his shoulders.

"Please?" He repeated, slipping another finger inside her. She bucked against him, hard, but her jeans were limiting her movement. He grinned and lifted her over his shoulder thinking that she was like his very own mermaid.

Only far, far more beautiful, and infinitely more dangerous.

His room was upstairs, but he was too impatient for that. He took her to his study instead, and lay her down on the rarely-used desk.

"This is cold," she surprised him by laughing.

Her laugh was a beautiful, sweet sound. Her face was beautiful and sweet too.

But she was not. At least, he was pretty sure she wasn't. The flash of doubt wasn't welcome. He disregarded it.

"You'll survive."

His tone was cold and it surprised her. She blinked up at him, but before she could question his meaning, he reached behind her and unclipped her bra, freeing her breasts into his broad hands. He held them and moved his body over hers, so that his arousal was intimately connected with her, despite the pants he wore.

Sophie lifted her hips, but her jeans were still wrapped around her ankles and she couldn't get as close to him as she wanted. She went to pull a leg free but he shook his head.

"No."

"No?" Her voice was puffed. She was breathless from desire.

He wanted to make love to her. He wanted to seduce her. He wanted to make her beg for him, over and over again.

He wanted her to fall in love with him.

To fall so hard, so spectacularly, that she would do anything he asked of her.

Including quit her job and never speak to Eric again.

His smile hid a cold sense of determination.

He undressed quickly, pausing only to protect them from unwanted consequences, and then he took possession of her body. She was ready for him, and yet when he swiftly pushed into her, she cried out. Her voice was a tremulous throb in the silence of his house.

"You are okay?" He checked, stroking her cheek.

Tears sparkled in her eyes and she nodded, dragging her lower lip between her teeth. Her cheeks were flushed. And as he looked into her face, he knew. No one had made her feel like that.

She was his already.

The power was a beast; a seductive mistress for it made him feel God-like.

He moved slowly, feeling his way, and watching her constantly, to see what pleased her most. When Sophie was almost manic with need, he stopped teasing her and returned to what she loved most.

She released herself almost instantly, and he held her while she fell apart, whispering words in his native tongue until she slowly regained her breathing. But he wasn't done with her yet. He began to move once more, thrusting powerfully into her, this time rough and hard, and she bucked even harder against him and screamed in surprised pleasure.

He dug his fingers into her buttocks and when she began to spiral out of control for a second time, he followed after her, releasing himself with a guttural cry.

Their breath combined in the air as a strangled sound of agreement.

That had been earth-shattering.

And for Alex, it had been necessary.

He had done it.

He had physically possessed her; but that wasn't enough. He needed all of her, for good, to make sure she would stay out of Helena's way. And so he did not pull away from her and put some distance between them, as he usually did with his conquests.

This was a game, and he had to play his part.

"You are every bit as perfect as I had hoped."

Sophie's eyes fluttered shut and she lifted a hand to her neck. The fingers were not steady and her throat was pink from his stubble. "I don't think I understand what just happened."

Sex. Sex had just happened. For the first time in her life, Sophie had just done something she'd always sworn she wouldn't. She'd slept with a man she knew nothing about, just because he was gorgeous. She'd thrown caution to the wind and … and … fucked. Or been fucked. She didn't know which.

"Oh, God." She covered both eyes with her hands and shook her head slowly from side to side. He was still inside of her, but mortification was beginning to take over any sense of lust she'd been indulging.

"Sophie, what is the matter?"

Even the way he said her name turned her insides to mush. She had never been so utterly vulnerable to a man as she was now, to this man.

"I can't believe that just happened." She kept her eyes shut beneath the veil of her hands. "What the hell was I thinking?"

"You weren't thinking," he teased. "You were feeling."

"Oh, stop. You're making it worse. Please, please get off me."

He laughed softly, but did as she'd requested.

"Oh, God."

Her guilt and shame were obvious, and he had a sinking feeling that he understood what motivated those emotions. She had, after all, just cheated on her lover. And it had been spectacular.

"What we did is not wrong, *agape mou*."

"Easy for you to say," she groaned. "You do this all the time."

He pushed aside the statement. "And you don't?"

"No!" She said it with such venom that he stilled. His hands were running down her arms, bringing her slowly back to life. But her guilt was too difficult to assuage. She was upset.

He sighed and did as she'd asked, moving away from her. The instantaneous emptiness that filled him was a surprise.

"You do not have sex?"

"No!" She shook her head, her eyes still winched shut.

"You were not a virgin." He grinned down at her, genuinely amused by the picture she made. Somehow he doubted she had any idea how utterly ravishing she looked, stretched naked across his desk with her eyes shut and her lips pouted.

"No, but I don't know you. I mean, I hardly know you. And you're just the kind of man I try to avoid."

Because I'm not married, he wondered bitterly. "What is it about me that you try to avoid?"

"Your *experience*." The way she said the word, an insult was obviously implied, but he couldn't fathom what it was.

"Did my *experience* displease you in some way?"

She risked blinking one eye open, and even with a single look was able to convey a sense of mockery. "This is not the time to seek praise for your skills."

"Ah," he shrugged. "You are wrong there. It is *always* the time for a man to be complimented on how well he makes love to a beautiful woman."

"Stop!" She closed both eyes again. "You're making it … So. Much. Worse."

She was the woman who was breaking up his sister's marriage and yet he felt a lovely kernel of pleasure at this unexpected conversation. He moved back to her and gently glided her jeans up her legs. "I do not know what you feel is bad about our situation, but I should like to have dinner with you while you try to explain it to me."

Sophie's sharp intake of breath showed her surprise. "You would?"

"*Ne.*"

"No?"

"*Ne* is yes," he admonished softly. "And if you are to raise two Greek boys, you should learn to speak some of the language." He gripped her hands and pulled her gently to standing. "I will teach you."

Her eyes were enormous, and she stared at his face as though she were drowning. "You will?" For that implied so much more than what she was expecting from him.

"*Ne,*" he grinned, and pressed a light kiss against the tip of her nose.

"Alex." But what did she want to say? What could she say? This was wrong. Or was it? It certainly felt a thousand shades of right. "What shall we eat?"

CHAPTER THREE

"*Two* sisters?" His look of disbelief was priceless. Then again, Alex had led his life to that point looking out for Helena. The idea of multiplying his worry and responsibilities was onerous indeed.

Sophie shook her head dolefully. "Not just two sisters. *Triplets.*"

"Triplets?" He expelled a long, slow whistle. "You mean somewhere in Australia there are two girls just as gorgeous as you walking around the outback?"

Sophie laughed. "No." The champagne was excellent; the food even more so. She'd always been a sucker for Indian and this little restaurant was the most authentic she'd tried. She fingered a pappadum thoughtfully. "We're not identical. Though if you saw us together, you'd know we were related. And as for the outback, Olivia and Ava wouldn't be seen dead there."

"Tell me about them."

Sophie screwed up her nose unconsciously as she thought of her sisters with the same lurching in her gut that always accompanied their absence. "They're the most amazing women you can possibly imagine."

"Really?" He reclined in his chair, his expression indomitable. It was very easy for Sophie to see him then as the powerful, dynamic megalomaniac who'd amassed a global empire all on his own.

"Really," she confirmed, ignoring her dry mouth and racing heart.

"How so?"

"They're just ... the kind of women that you look at and think 'wow'." He looked at her with an expression of doubt. Did Sophie not know that she was similarly impressive?

"Olivia is the flighty one. She's beautiful and popular and footloose and fancy-free. She travels on a whim. She's truly ..."

"Amazing?" He supplied with a teasing grin.

She nodded and sipped her water.

"What about the other one?"

Sophie smiled when she thought of Ava. "Far more serious. Then again, she's the responsible one. Despite the fact we're triplets, Ava has always seemed older. She's felt very free to boss Liv and me around from day one." She shrugged. "But we're happy to let her. She's holding the business together at home now, while Olivia and I get to travel and have fun."

"The business?"

Sophie's eyes assumed a faraway expression. "Casa Celli." She sighed wistfully. "Our vineyard."

"I don't see you as the agricultural type."

She smiled distractedly. "I'm not. Hence my itchy feet as soon as I left school." She shrugged. "But we grew up on the property. Mum ran it and produced some fantastic vintages before she ... before we lost her."

Something like pain sharpened inside his gut. Alex ignored it. "When did she die?"

Sophie winced. "I'm sorry. I don't think like that. Even now I find it hard to accept that she's gone." She shook her head wistfully. "It was five years ago this Christmas."

"How?" Ever the businessman, he was focussed on the information he could obtain.

"When mum wasn't checking the vines for pests and sugar, she was diving." When he didn't speak, she continued, though she couldn't meet his eyes for they reflected her own pain too clearly. "Our vineyards slope all the way to the sea. It's the most stunning piece of land on Earth. I can't begin to explain the glory and goodness of those hills." She smiled as she recalled her youth. "My sisters and I used to run amongst the vines for hours on end, building cubby houses and pretending we were wayward fairies on our way to the faraway tree. It was an air-bubble-childhood."

Alex linked his fingers with hers. "An air bubble? What does this mean?"

Sophie flickered her gaze to his chiselled face and then turned her focus back to the pappadum. "You know, an air bubble. Like life is the water and our childhood was that single, miraculous bubble, floating indefatigably amongst it. We were immune from everything. Sadness, responsibility, grief and worry."

He didn't speak, but his dark eyes urged her to continue. "Mum was magical all the time, but at Christmas, she was like an angel on earth." Her smile was unknowingly enigmatic. "She spent months preparing. We didn't have a lot of money, growing up, so she'd have to order our presents early. They were never extravagant. Just a book we wanted or maybe a special dress." She shrugged. "We'd decorate the tree together, all four of us. It would take a whole day and we'd listen to carols, singing along as we hung all of our favourite pieces." Her fingers toyed with her hair. "Mum was American, and she'd brought a heap of very old ornaments over with her. They were glass, and so beautiful and fragile that they still make me all gooey to think of them today."

"Gooey?" He teased.

"You know. Heart rushing, excited. There were a million little things she did that made it the most beautiful time of year."

"What else?" It fascinated him, for his own life had been devoid of such traditions.

"Well, we had a pudding recipe that would knock your socks off. So much rum and port, with fruit mince and figs. It was rich and heavy and oh so good. My sisters and I would huddle around mum while she made it, begging for tastes from the spoon."

He laughed softly at the memory. "And when she boiled it, the whole house would smell like Christmas. For days and days we'd joke that we were living in a cinnamon cloud."

He nodded, and so she continued. "We'd make a gingerbread house every year. We started off making just one. When we were young, mum would dig out the stencil and we'd sit around the table while she cut the pieces. But then, as we got older, we each tried our hand at making our own house. Eventually, it became a competition, and mum would judge the winner."

"And did you all win?"

"Oh, no. Mum wasn't one of those 'please everyone' new-age parents. She genuinely judged based on merit. Which meant I never won."

He laughed again. "Why not?"

"Are you kidding? I'd eaten half the house by the time I got to stick it together. I am a sucker for gingerbread. The less baked the better. In fact, it would probably be my desert island food."

"A gingerbread house?"

"Nope. Gingerbread dough. Unbaked. Cold and smooshy."

"That sounds ... disgusting."

"You wait. I'll make it for you one day."

Something odd flushed through him at the easy way she threw such promises around.

He covered it quickly with another question. "Who made the best gingerbread houses?"

"Ava," she responded immediately. "I can still picture her, sitting up late measuring the walls to within a millimetre. She'd bake spare slabs in case any developed cracks. She is very precise."

"She sounds it."

Sophie sighed. "And on Christmas morning, we'd wake up to the smell of baked ham and scrambled eggs, and croissants with cheese. Mum was a wonderful cook. Looking back, it must have been exhausting, but she always swore she loved it." Sophie's smile was bitter-sweet. "That was mum, though. She was determined that we would have a happy, uneventful life."

"A true opposite to my own childhood, then." He'd spoken without thinking. He never, without exception, spoke of his youth.

But Sophie was fast. "In what way?"

"We are not talking about me," he attempted to demur, but she wasn't going to let it pass so easily.

"No, but I'd like to. I presume you mean you were the water. Or at least, that you were flotsam on the water. Rather than the air-bubble," she clarified, at his lost expression.

He couldn't help but smile at her quick turn of phrase. "If you exchange water for sludge, then yes. I was detritus in the mud of life, during my childhood."

She squeezed his fingers. "I am tempted to say that it can't have been so bad, except that I suspect you are not prone to exaggeration."

"No," he admitted grimly. "It was more dire that I would admit to most people."

"How?" She pushed, in the same demanding way he had employed.

And though he'd brought her to his house to seduce her, and though he believed he had every reason to distrust her, he heard himself say, "It would be impossible to describe."

Sophie lifted his hand above the table and unfurled his fingers. She placed a kiss in his palm and then closed his fist back up. "I *want* to know more."

An exasperated noise escaped his throat without his consent. "I'm not sure it would do any good to speak of it."

"But would it do any harm?"

He studied her carefully. "You might think less of me."

Sophie pulled a face. "If you truly believe I am the kind of woman to judge someone on their background or the way they were raised then you don't know me at all." She flushed to the roots of her pale, silky hair. "You *don't* know me at all. Not really. So let me tell you something. I don't really care about where you've come from, except in so much as it changes who you are now. If you don't want to talk about it, I'll let it go. But if you're hiding it from me because you're ashamed, then I'm going to be very offended."

A long beat of silence throbbed between them before Alex found his voice. "You seem to have an ability to unsettle and surprise me."

"I try hard," she teased with a shrug of her shoulders.

"It is not something my lovers usually care to discuss."

And in a flash, the atmosphere began to crackle with tension. It zapped around them, and Sophie didn't know where to look. Despite the crowd in the restaurant, they were alone, and her chest was hurting.

"What do they want to discuss?" She managed through half-gritted teeth.

"Sophie." He sighed. "We have gone off-course."

"Have we?" She simpered, biting into the pappadum and swallowing the piece whole.

"You were telling me about your air-bubble."

She lifted her water and sipped it slowly. It wasn't his fault that her emotions were zipping all over the place. Something had slipped loose in her usual resolve and now it was up to Sophie to pick up the pieces.

"It was my mother's doing. She was determined that we would enjoy a beautiful youth."

"Why?"

"Because she never had one," Sophie said simply. "Her parents were poor, and she had to get a job when she was young. She grew up in Manhattan and she got a part time job in a record store, but it took her almost an hour to get there on three different busses. As soon as she found out she was pregnant with us, she drove off into the sunset."

"To Australia? That seems ... both drastic and brave."

"Yes to both. That was my mum though. Brave and fearless, and determined as hell." She sipped on her soda water, and told herself that the burning in her throat came from the bubbles and not the cloying threat of tears. "She was diving when she died." Her eyes were prickling with the sting of unshed salt. "Countless people have said to me, 'at least she died doing something she loved'."

Alex made a sound of frustration. "A pointless platitude. Far better to live and spend many more years doing what she loved than to die needlessly."

Sophie's heart turned over in her chest. "Yes, exactly. That is exactly as I feel. It almost seems worse that we lost her to diving. As though one of her great loves betrayed her."

He pushed his sympathy deep down in his gut. He didn't want to feel it for this woman. He couldn't forget, no matter how enchanting her stories were, that she was a danger to him, for she was a danger to his sister.

"And your father?" He enquired silkily.

Sophie shrugged. "We never knew him."

"Never? He chose not to be in your lives?"

"Apparently." She bit down on her lip, a habit of hers he found distracting to the extreme.

"You've never contacted him?"

"No."

"You don't want him in your life." A statement, not a question.

"I don't know how to contact him," she corrected, careful to keep emotion flattened from her tone.

"What do you mean?" His eyes narrowed as he studied her.

"Whoever he is, he wanted no part of mum when she told him she was pregnant. From what we know, which isn't a lot, he paid her off to stay out of his life and keep quiet."

Something like anger rolled through Alex. Anger at this man? At his lack of integrity? "How old was your mother?"

"Twenty four. My age."

"A baby."

"Hardly. How old are you?"

His laugh was a rich sound. "Thirty four."

"A decade between us." She reclined in her chair and studied his face. He had an ageless quality to him. Skin that was flawlessly tanned and eyes that were mysterious and loaded with emotion. "You are older than Helena," Sophie said, moving her hands to her lap and clasping them there.

At the mention of his sister, Alex seemed to stiffen momentarily. "*Ne.*"

Her pulse fired in response to his sexy utterance. It reminded her of the way he'd whispered foreign words into her mouth while they made love. She dipped her eyes away.

"Helena is only a few years older than you."

"And yet you're very close."

"On what do you base this conclusion?"

"I've seen you together. I have two sisters, remember? Sisters I'm close to. I understand the dynamic. The dependence. The silent ability we have of communicating to one another that baffles outsiders." Her smile was richly enigmatic and his desire kicked up a notch.

"Is this how it is between us?"

"Between *us?*"

"Between Helena and me," he clarified with a tight smile.

"Oh." Her cheeks burned and she rolled her eyes, embarrassed by her own wishful stupidity. "Yes. She looks at you and it's as though she's spoken. You get her."

"In a way her husband doesn't?" He prompted silkily.

"Oh." Sophie was stricken. "That's not really my place to say." Her words all rushed together, and though Alex's English was impeccable, he had to concentrate to decipher them through her accent and haste.

"You are uniquely placed to say," he corrected.

Sophie forced her gaze to meet his, and her heart kicked in her chest. He was so beautiful. So breath-takingly stunning. "What are you really asking me?"

Did she suspect that he knew? Or did she know that he suspected? He brushed his foot against hers beneath the table, enjoying the way her eyes widened instantly at the surprise contact.

"My sister was very young when she married Eric. He is ambitious. I wonder sometimes if he is making her happy."

Eric's worry that Alex would interfere in his marriage came to the fore of her mind. And yet what could Sophie say? To deny that Helena was miserable didn't sit comfortably with her. Her breathing was shallow; her lungs seemed to burn with confusion. "Working in someone's house requires a level of discretion. I'm there, but I'm not there. And I'm certainly not there to judge, nor gossip."

"Gossip," he refuted with a sharp laugh. "I am her brother. Eric is my friend."

"Yes," she nodded, but her eyes glinted with determination. "And I'm sure they would both appreciate my discretion."

"You are discreet as a matter of course then?" He asked, thinking of what a necessary quality that would be in conducting an affair with her married employer.

"Of course. It goes with the job."

Alex felt frustration licking at his heels. He had bet on bedding her, but not on finding her this fascinating. He had also not imagined she might prove so difficult to comprehend.

"You're very protective of her."

"Helena?" Alex clarified, pausing while the waiter served their main course. The delicious aroma of curries and accompaniments surrounded them and Sophie inhaled gratefully.

When he began speaking, she'd almost forgotten what she'd asked. "My own parents died when I was eleven. Helena was four."

"Oh, Alex. I'm so sorry."

"We had no other family. My parents were very happy, but very poor. Our apartment was tiny and rented. We were evicted the day after the funeral."

"That's terrible. I'm so sorry," she said again, for want of anything else she could possibly say.

He smiled dismissively. "We were put into foster care." He compressed his lips and wondered why he was telling Sophie this. He had never spoken of that torrid time in his life to another soul. He had kept it out of the press. It was his silent shame and personal pain. Did he want her to feel guilt? To pity the woman she was wounding with her callous cheating? "But the parents were … let us just say they epitomised the worst of the system." His smile was grim.

"I'm so sorry." She seemed to be repeating herself, but the thought of two such young siblings going through what he was describing sent a shiver down her spine.

"We ran away. Or rather, I ran away, and dragged Helena after me."

"What did you do?" She was transfixed.

"We lived rough for several years. There is a big gypsy population in Athens and they were kind to us. I worked for them."

"But what about school? Didn't you have school?"

"Not for many years. I didn't feel comfortable to leave Helena for long. Though we found friends on the street, she was young and always very trusting. I lived in fear of her being taken." Indeed, his face paled at the recollection of the worry he'd carried for so long.

"So you see, Sophie," her name was a caress on his chiselled lips, "I have spent my life protecting Helena. It comes naturally to me to enquire as to her well-being."

Sophie, in that moment, longed to confide her own worries in him. For Helena was not happy. She was not well. And no one was prepared to face the truth of that. The burden of being the only one who truly appreciated her illness was heavy to carry.

Only Eric's plea kept her silent.

He was married to Helena, and Helena loved him. She'd chosen to make a life with him, and have children with him. Surely Eric's wishes trumped Alex's?

She swallowed. "How did you get out of that life?"

He noticed the way she'd deflected his question, but he allowed it to pass. His eyes assumed a faraway look as he reflected on that fateful time. "When I was fifteen, I broke into one of the mansions in the centre of the city." He shook his head ruefully. "Up until then, I'd stolen wallets from tourists and food from restaurants, but never anything more ambitious. Those houses though ..." He shrugged his broad shoulders and laughed, though it had been a desperate, hungry time in his life. "It was to be my first and last house burglary."

"What happened?" She was, quite literally, on the edge of her seat. The thought of food was forgotten.

"It was the home of Pierre Lisoura; perhaps you have heard of him?"

"The guy who owns the airline?"

"The very same." He nodded. "He was in his sixties then, but he was not afraid of me. He could have taken me to the police and had me charged. I do not know why he chose not to."

"What did he do instead?"

"He made me work for him. He told me he'd give me a job for as long as I went to school."

"And Helena?"

"She was old enough for school by then, too. He helped me to enrol us, and he hired tutors to catch me up. Instead of giving me money, he rented a small flat for us, and made sure we had enough to eat. And after school, I would go to his house, and work until late at night."

"What kind of things would you do for him?"

"Menial work initially. At the time, that is what I thought at least. But now I realise he was always teaching me. He allowed me to pour coffee while he had meetings; he asked me to type notes for him on top level negotiations. He noticed early on that I had a keen interest in finance and corporate acquisitions and he began to include me in more and more of this kind of work."

"A perfect benefactor for a man such as you."

"An angel sent from the heavens; for without him, I would probably be dead or in jail."

A shiver ran down Sophie's spine. "Was it horrible?"

"The streets? Not as awful as foster care," he denied with a tight smile.

"You are still living proof that miracles happen. To have turned your life around like that ... I'm in awe, frankly."

Yes, he was proof that miracles happened. It was amazing that a street kid like him had climbed the corporate ranks to become almost sickeningly wealthy. "You never really shake it though."

"What's that?"

"The looking over your shoulder, waiting for something bad to happen."

The searingly honest statement was news to him. Alex shifted uncomfortably in his seat. He would have said, until that moment, that he'd dumped the ghosts of his youth many moons ago. So why was he professing something different to this woman?

It occurred to him that she was one of the *seirenes*; the sirens, a mythical creature who existed purely to lure men upon the craggy rocks of the islands. She spoke, and it was as if she was singing a song only he heard; was it leading him to his own destruction, like the myths forewarned?

No! Alessandros could have laughed at the ludicrously indulgent pondering. She was no siren. She was a woman. A sexy, beautiful, undoubtedly self-interested woman. He studied her through narrowed eyes. Even her willingness to sleep with him showed her mercenary spirit. For though Eric was moderately wealthy and had aspirations to political power, he was nothing to Alessandros. That was not hubris nor vanity speaking. If Alex had any doubts as to his own power and success, he could not have borne it long in the face of the articles that had been run about him.

Gut instinct and self-confidence had done that. He would not let himself doubt those gifts now.

Helena worried that her husband was cheating, and now Alex knew for certain that he was. He would have put every penny he owned on a bet that something was going on between Sophie and Eric.

He smiled at her, but the pleasure was all for himself. Helena was going to be okay. Her marriage would survive this.

Because he would not allow Sophie to be a problem.

* * *

9 August, 11.08pm
From: Sophie
To: Ava, Olivia

Well, girls.
I've gone and done something really, drastically dense.
There! I've said it first, so neither of you needs to bother telling me that I've taken leave of my senses.

Do you remember I've told you about my bosses? Helena and Eric? Well, Helena's brother's in town at the moment. She paused typing for a moment, so that she could catch her breath. Back in her own bedroom, in the small room between the twins' rooms, the whole affair felt almost like a dream. But it wasn't! Three glorious nights, and Sophie knew. Her fingers flew over the keyboard as she forced herself to put into writing what she hadn't dared admit to herself. *And I've fallen completely head over heels in love with him.*

Okay, I can hear you rolling your eyes, Ava. I know just what you'd say. It's not possible to love someone you barely know.

But I do know him. I know so much about him ... we've talked and talked and talked until our words clog the air. We talk about everything and nothing and I fall asleep wishing I could hear more.

I don't know what's going to happen. I don't even know how long he's planning to stay in London. He's ... what? A billionaire? A mogul? A tycoon? She ground her teeth together and waded back into the email. *Pretty busy, I think, so I guess he'll have to go soon.*

Anyway, I didn't want to say anything before now, because I wasn't sure it was real. But it is. It definitely is.

I miss you both.

Lots of love, S.

She pressed send and curled her knees up under her chin. The evening was warm – at least for London – and she was wearing only a simple cotton nightgown.

Was he still in the house? Her heart fluttered as she imagined him, somewhere there, his body warm, his arms strong. He'd taken coffee with Helena after they got back; a habit that Sophie didn't personally appreciate. Coffee so late in the evening would have kept her awake.

And Sophie hadn't wanted to intrude on their family time, anyway. When he took her away, to his house, or out on dates, they were 'them'. Sophie and Alex, rapidly becoming an actual couple, despite the fact it had been less than a week since they had met.

But here, at No. 11 Herringbone Lane, Sophie was the children's nanny first and foremost. The moment she began sitting around sipping drinks with Helena, Eric and Alex, was the moment the lines would be blurred in an odd way.

Yet Alex seemed to try to push it. To encourage her to sit with him even when she was obviously not prepared for that. Not prepared for the possible questions from Eric and Helena, either.

A noise sounded on her iPad. She flicked it open and grinned when she saw two new emails – one from each of her sisters. She opened Ava's first.

9 August, 11.10pm
From: Ava
To: Sophie, Olivia

Sophie, no! What are you talking about? What's the first thing mum taught us about love?

9 August, 11.11pm
From: Olivia
To: Ava, Sophie

Oh my God! Tell me more! Send a pic! How very, very exciting! O.x

Sophie laughed at their different responses and was about to write something back when another email pinged through.

9 August, 11.12pm
From: Olivia
To: Ava, Sophie

Ava Anne Henderson, don't be such a misanthrope. What mum would or wouldn't say isn't important here. What matters is that our sister is in love with a man, for the first time in her life. Why can't you be supportive of that?

9 August, 11.14pm
From: Sophie
To: Ava, Olivia

It's okay, guys. Liv, I know Ava's just looking out for me. And she's right. You know she is. Mum learned her lesson the hard way and wanted us all to avoid the same fate. No way am I going to end up pregnant to this guy. And he's nothing like our father. Or what we know of him, anyway. He was a jerk. A first grade a-hole who ditched a pregnant woman because he was married.

Alex is wonderful. I could write pages and pages and pages telling you how amazing he is, but you still wouldn't get it. He's just ... perfect.

I love him.

And I know you're worried about me, Ava, because that's what you do. But you don't need to be.

Have you ever met someone and just known*? That though it doesn't make sense, and there are a million and one reasons to be cautious and go slowly, you just simply can't? Because you trust that person, and you need that person, and you loved that person, from the first moment you met them ...? That's how it is with us. I'd trust him with my life.*

I love him.

Okay, on that sappy note, it's late here. I need to sleep. Don't argue over this. It's a good thing. Trust me. You'll see.

Xxx

She flicked her iPad into flight mode to avoid the barrage of emails that she was certain would follow and fell back onto the bed. Her smile was enormous on her face.

She was crazy! The whole thing was crazy!

A knock sounded at her door and she pushed up onto her elbows, her heart immediately beginning to pound as she prepared for the sight of Alex.

Only it was Eric instead.

"Sorry to intrude," he murmured in that terribly British way he had. There was something indefinably Hugh Grant about him that always made her smile.

"You're not," she lied, crossing her legs at her ankles and smoothing her nightgown down past her knees. "Is it the twins? Are they okay?"

"Yes," he waved a hand in the air dismissively and sat on the foot of the bed. "We were talking the other day and we got cut off."

"We were?" She searched her memory and found only Alex. Little fragments of recollection of their time together that were too pleasurable to sweep past. Walks to his house, and through his house, cups of tea on his terrace and long, passionate love-making in his enormous bed.

"Soph?"

"Oh!" She felt her cheeks burn and shook her head. "Sorry. You were saying?"

"No," he had a slightly teasing tone to his voice. "*You* were saying, yesterday, something about Christmas and the twins."

"Oh!" She nodded jerkily. "Of course." How had she forgotten? "I hate asking you this," she said hurriedly, and she truly did. "But I want to get them something special for Christmas. There's a performance at the Royal Albert Hall, only tickets are ..." Her blush deepened. "Well, they're almost a week's pay for me. I wondered if you'd ..."

"Of course I'll buy the tickets, Sophie. You don't even need to ask."

"No!" She shook her head, consternation making her eyes wide. "I want to buy them. It's a gift from me. Only they go on sale this weekend and if I don't book right away they'll likely sell out. I was just wondering if you'd mind ... loaning me the money, until then."

"I'd feel awful for you to be out of pocket ..."

"Please, I want to give the tickets to the boys. Only I'm stretched now..."

"Of course." The Aussie dollar being what it was, it was not hard to believe she'd found her money didn't go so far. And the salary nannies earned was hardly salubrious.

"You just tell me how much and I'll have it for you tomorrow."

"Thank you." She named an amount and shook her head. "I'm so embarrassed to have to even ask you."

"Sophie, you love my children. What more could I ask for? We are lucky to have you. I'm lucky to have you."

He stood and moved towards the door. Sophie followed him, simply because it felt like the polite thing to do. "Eric?" She said as he pulled it inwards. "Can we keep this between us?" She was thinking of Alex, of course, and how he might try to loan her money if he knew how dire her finances were.

"Our little secret," he grinned and tapped a finger under her chin. "We won't tell a soul."

She laughed gratefully, and then a movement behind him caught her gaze.

Alex. Dark. Menacing. And watchful. A shiver ran down her spine as, for the first time since meeting him, she felt a coldness in him that was capable of freezing her core.

It was covered over almost instantly, smoothed away into a façade of bland disinterest, so that she presumed she'd imagined it.

"Alex. You off, mate?"

He looked at Eric for a long, cold moment, waiting for the urge to punch his friend's handsome face to subside. And then, behind him was Sophie. Beautiful, treacherous Sophie who controlled his dreams and waking thoughts. Sophie whom he had intended to seduce and pull away from his sister's home and then discard, who had worked her way into his being and become a necessary component to his existence. She was a drug and yet he was no better nor happier than a heroine addict.

"Soon. I came to say goodnight to Sophie."

"Right-o. I'll see you tomorrow. Night, Soph."

Eric walked down the stairs, whistling a tune, his manner happy. Satisfied?

Possessive fury burned through Alex.

His eyes raked over Sophie from head to toe, pausing on the swell of her breasts that was obvious beneath the flimsy night gown. Had Eric ... had he ... had they?

Alex banked down on the horrible imagery. He had come to London with the intention of investigating matters, and now he couldn't bear thinking about Sophie with another man.

It couldn't be true, because he couldn't bear it to be.

"Alex? Are you okay?"

"No," he said honestly. His dark eyes were glowing in his chiselled face, putting Sophie in mind of the darkest night skies.

"What is it?" She moved to him instinctively and lifted a hand to his broad chest. She could feel his heart pounding beneath her touch.

"I need to know."

Sophie nodded slowly, though she couldn't fathom what he was talking about. "Need to know what?"

Her face was beautiful; there was no denying it. But it wasn't just a physical attractiveness that made him stare. It was her manner. So open and genuine, he found it almost impossible to believe that she was undermining his sister. Was it possible Helena and he had erred?

But why had Eric been visiting her so late in the evening? In her bedroom, while she was wearing practically nothing. He swallowed away the bitterness and forced a smile to his face.

"I just met you."

"Yes," she agreed, her expression quizzical.

"But I've bought companies in the space of hours. I've always listened to my instincts."

Though she had no idea where he was going, Sophie's heart began to race in her chest. "Yes?"

"And every fibre of my being is telling me that I'll regret it for the rest of my life if I don't ask you to marry me."

The silence pulsed between them, heavy with shock and surprise. "Marry you?" Sophie finally broke it, her voice squeaky in the night air.

"Yes. Marry me."

Her mouth gaped. She looked down the hallway, as if just remembering where they were. She pulled him into her bedroom and quietly clicked the door closed behind them.

"I'm sorry," she spoke quietly, and Alex had a surge of panic. She was going to say *no*, and it would all be over.

He waited silently for her to finish her sentence, but he was far from patient. Inside, he was a ticking bomb.

"I don't think I heard you properly. I do that sometimes. I vague out and fantasize." She shook her head in a gesture that he found frustratingly adorable. "What did you say?"

Relief was spreading through him. "You heard perfectly, *agape mou*. Marry me."

"I thought that's what you said." Her tongue darted out and licked her lower lip. "It's so sudden."

He laughed softly and linked his arms behind her back, pulling her against his broad frame. "Marry me."

"But you live in Greece."

His nod was droll. "And you're from Australia. These are details, not significant factors."

She made a chortling sound. "Easy for you to say."

"Marry me."

She stared at him with a strange, drowning sensation. "But why?"

"Because every fibre of my being tells me it is right for us to marry. And I believe you feel the same way."

Their eyes clashed, and understanding throbbed between them.

"Okay."

"Okay?" He laughed into her cheek and then kissed her.

"Yes! Of course, yes!"

* * *

The packet was waiting for him when he got home. It must have arrived with the day's post, and he'd shuffled it all onto his desk for later attention.

Proposing to Sophie Henderson had taken the focus out of his mind for a moment. After all, it had surprised him as much as it had her.

But it had been the right call.

He would never know for sure if she and Eric were carrying on an affair, and how serious it was, but there was enough proof to have him seriously concerned. As his wife, she would be out of the picture.

She would be his. And only his.

A tight smile of anticipation spread across his features as he thought of long, Greek nights at his home on Corfu. How he would enjoy teasing her delectable body when she was fully his. No imperative to return her to the house on Herringbone Lane; he would take all night to pleasure her and take his pleasure from her.

His body tightened at the very idea.

He slipped his finger beneath the flap of the envelope carelessly, and dropped the papers onto his desk.

The report was about twenty pages long.

And it contained the information he had dreaded.

Sophie Henderson, formerly employed by a Sir Edwin Thomas of Sydney, Australia, had been, according to various sources, involved in an affair with her married employer. The wife had fired her as soon as she found out. The words in front of his eyes were black and white.

His fingers were unsteady as he siphoned through the papers until he found a photograph of the man in question. Balding, overweight, with a personal fortune in the tens of millions, it was not difficult to see what the appeal had been.

So, Sophie had form for hitting on her wealthy employers, did she?

Was it money she sought? Or was she one of those women who simply liked to torment other women? To snag other women's husbands for personal satisfaction?

He cast the papers aside with a groan and leaned back in his chair. What had he expected? He'd come here fully believing her capable of such behaviour. And now? Proof of yet another affair shouldn't have shocked him. And yet it did.

CHAPTER FOUR

10 August, 06.11 am
From: Ava
To: Sophie, Olivia

Good Lord, Sophie. Marriage?
To this guy??

10 August, 06.12 am
From: Olivia
To: Sophie, Ava

It's not 'this guy', Aves, she loves him. He loves her. Does the fact it's all happened really quickly make it less likely to be good for her?

10 August, 06.13 am
From: Ava
To: Sophie, Olivia

YES!!!!!

Sophie read the emphatic reply with a smile on her lips; it was a smile that had been in place since agreeing to marry him.

Alessandros Petrides.

All night, she'd smiled into her pillow and dreamed of her future. A future with this Greek god of a man by her side, and one day perhaps, bonny little children playing at her feet.

10 August, 06.15 am
From: Sophie

To: Ava, Olivia

I love him. I know it must seem crazy impulsive, but I <u>*really*</u> *love him. I'm not going to love him more or less or differently if we wait six months, nor if we wait a year. I love him. It's that simple. I don't have any doubts about marrying him. Please be happy for me. X*

10 August, 06.16 am
From: Ava
To: Sophie, Olivia

You think that now, because you're in the first fog of love and lust.
And it's natural that you'd feel that way.
But what damage does it do to be really <u>sure</u>?
I don't want you getting hurt, and men like AP are ... well ... not the safest bet. If he loves you, he'll wait.

10 August, 06.17 am
From: Sophie
To: Ava, Olivia

He's not Cristiano.

She sent it and then immediately wished she could pull the email back through cyber-space. Her stomach swirled as she regretted instantly writing the three words that must surely have caused Ava a river of pain. She chewed on her lower lip and hovered her fingers over the keyboard. But what could she say to undo her snappy reply? Invoking the memory of Cristiano Cesar Barata had been a very, very low blow.

Time seemed to stretch like a piece of elastic that wouldn't snap. Sophie sat in her bed, her iPad beside her, guilt lurching through her system.

10 August, 06.25 am
From: Sophie
To: Ava, Olivia

I'm sorry. I know you're just worried about me. That wasn't fair.

It's just ... Alex is an amazing guy. He makes me ridiculously happy.

How's Milly?

10 August, 06.26 am
From: Ava
To: Sophie, Olivia

She's fine.

Adorable.

Missing you both.

Cristiano is coming back to town in November for Tom Berry's wedding.

10 August, 06.27 am
From: Olivia
To: Sophie, Ava

WHAT!!!! Hang on a sec. I just got back to my room and there's like a million messages from you two. Let me catch up.

Ava, Sophie's right. When you know, you know. If you're sure he's the right one, then I'm happy for you. I can't make the wedding, given that you two are in such a huge rush, but I was thinking I could stop over in Greece on my way to Vegas?! Let me know if that works for you.

Meanwhile, what the hell do you mean, 'Cristiano is coming back'? Isn't that sort of a disaster?

10 August, 06.28 am

From: Ava
To: Sophie, Olivia

I don't see why it needs to be.

10 August, 06.29 am
From: Olivia
To: Sophie, Ava

Um, maybe because of a rather adorable two year old with enormous brown eyes and olive skin? A little girl who is the spitting image of her father?

If Olivia could have known the effect her words had on Ava, she would have couched her point a little more carefully. For faraway, on the western edge of the Australian continent, surrounded by pristine grapevines and the sound of the rolling ocean in the distance, Ava was panicking. She had been panicking for months. The bridal party had booked to stay at her accommodation, the sweet little row of cottages nestled in amongst the grapes. And Ava had taken the booking before she'd realised that Cris would be one of their group. Her past, the past she'd spent every day facing up to because of their secret daughter, was about to come right back into her present.

10 August, 06.29 am
From: Ava
To: Sophie, Olivia

I'll work it out.

10 August, 06.30 am
From: Sophie
To: Ava, Olivia

You have to tell him, Aves. He's her dad. And he's going to take one look at her and know that.

10 August, 06.31 am
From: Ava
To: Sophie, Olivia

We weren't talking about me. Don't worry about Cristiano. I'll handle him.
Do you think either of you will make it for Christmas? I know you said you weren't sure ... but we'd love to see you.

It brought a nostalgic smile to Sophie's face. She hadn't even thought about Christmas. She had been planning to fly back for a whirlwind week. But that was before meeting Alessandro. Her heart clenched in her chest as she thought of her fiancé .

10 August, 06.32 am
From: Sophie
To: Ava, Olivia

I really don't know, I'm so sorry. If not this year, definitely next.
Liv, keep me posted on your plans. Would love to see you in Greece if you can make it. Ava, we need to talk more about Cris. I'll call you later in the week. Love you girls. x

10 August, 06.32 am
From: Olivia
To: Ava, Sophie

You go marry that gorgeous billionaire, Soph!! Have a champas for me and I'll see you soon. You're going to be a gorgeous bride.

* * *

"It's paradise," she said honestly.

"And yet you are quiet."

She bit down on her lip, her eyes following the coastline beneath Alex's enormous villa. "A little."

"What is it?" He lowered the spaghetti straps of her travelling dress and ran his hands over her bare shoulders. She was warmed from the sun and when he kissed her, he tasted sunshine mingled with perspiration and sunscreen.

"It's ... the boys," she said finally. "I can't help thinking about their little faces when we drove off."

Alex compressed his lips. No. Nor could he. Nor could he stop seeing Eric's slightly panicked expression as they stepped into the limousine. Only Helena had been truly happy. Relieved, even.

He pushed aside those thoughts. He was here now, with Sophie. His wife.

"Are you disappointed your sisters were not there?"

"Disappointed? Of course not." She spun around in the circle of his arms and smiled up at him. It was a convincing smile. He could genuinely believe that she loved him. "We hardly gave them time to make the trip, after all."

Two weeks! Who would have thought it could be arranged so swiftly? She stifled a perplexed sigh.

Alessandros Petrides could accomplish anything in the world, even a super-rushed wedding.

"Still, family is family. Perhaps we should have waited ..."

"Is that really what you would have wanted?" She teased, for his impatient streak had become a running joke between them.

"No. In fact, I would have dispatched my jet to collect them and refused to take no for an answer. I am pleased you are not sad they missed things."

"We'll see them soon. Ava's ... flat out on the ... vineyard at the moment." The small omission came surprisingly easily to her. Her husband would, one day, learn the truth about Ava, but the secret they'd all kept for so long was a habit Sophie wasn't yet ready to break. She skimmed over the statement; it was something she would discuss with him later. It wasn't a big deal anyway, to anyone but Ava, and the sisters who had helped her through the crisis of finding herself pregnant and alone. But with Cristiano's return to the vineyard on the horizon, Sophie couldn't help but feel a sense of worry as to how it would all work out.

"And Olivia's on one of her hair-brained trips."

"Hair-brained trips?" He prompted, already understanding the dynamic between the sisters despite having never so much as spoken to them.

"Liv likes to take off a few times a year. She's got a horde of equally crazy girlfriends and she chooses whomever is at a loose end at the same time and off they go. Travel on a shoe-string budget, live like a local. She'll write a guide book one day."

"Perhaps one of her next trips will be to Greece."

"She said the very same thing," Sophie agreed, wrinkling her nose. "But she's just as likely to change her mind tomorrow. She's a free spirit."

Alex nodded slowly. "I hope she makes the time for you. I would like to meet her, Mrs Petrides."

The wedding had passed in a blur. A beautiful intimate ceremony, followed by dinner at a phenomenal restaurant Sophie had only read about in Vogue and Harpers and Queen. And then this. An escape to his divine Greek mansion.

"This place is a palace," she said with a small smile.

"Your palace," he murmured, and her heart turned over. His expression was difficult to comprehend; it was as though he was waiting for her to say something. She shifted uncomfortably.

After all, she'd have done anything to have successfully avoided falling in love with a man with money and this kind of property at his fingertips. A man like her father had been.

Of the few facts they had about him, that he was a wealthy Italian was at the forefront of her mind often. And now she'd fallen in love with a super wealthy guy from a stunning Mediterranean island. Like she'd sworn she never would.

"Careful, I'll start demanding you address me as *Your Majesty*."

"I would call you anything you asked of me, Mrs Petrides."

Mrs Petrides. What a beautiful sound that had to it!

"Would you do anything I asked of you, too?" She said with a small smile.

"Well," his voice was throaty. "That depends on what it is."

She pulled at her dress, unzipping it at the side so that it floated down her body and she could step out of it easily. She wore the lacy white underpants the stylist had delivered, and no bra. "I saw a pool when we drove up. Is it private?"

"*Ne*," his eyes glittered as he allowed himself the pleasure of looking at her.

"Excellent. Swim with me."

"It would be my pleasure, *Your Majesty*," he teased.

Sophie's heart turned over. It had been a whirlwind, all right, but that didn't make it any less right nor perfect. Life had a habit of throwing curve balls and there was no way she was going to be foolish enough to pass this one up. What should she have done? Waited a sensible period of time as Ava had urged? For once, she was channelling her inner Olivia, and throwing any kind of caution to the wind.

"I'm so glad I married you," she said with a spark of pleasure as she stared up at him.

His eyes widened with apparent surprise and then he leaned down and scooped her up, carrying her small frame easily over one shoulder.

"Hey!" She laughed, punching him playfully. "I can walk you know."

"You walk beautifully, my love, but this way I get to touch you as we go." And to prove his point, he moved his hands to her rear, and cupper her buttocks.

But Sophie didn't react at first. She was momentarily struck by a dawning realisation.

My love. It had sounded strangely discordant and unusual coming from his mouth, and she immediately understood why.

He had never said that word to her. Or specifically, those three words. Had she said it to him? She searched her mind and recalled having uttered *I love you* several times, often after they'd made love and she was in the throes of falling back to earth after an unimaginable pleasure. But she'd said it at other times, too. When they were discussing the wedding and where they'd live initially. When they were walking hand and hand from his house to Helena's. She'd said it often.

And he hadn't.

He eased her down to the ground, his hands running over her body with possessive intent. "You are beautiful." It was a growl from the base of his throat; a deep sound laced with admiration and disbelief.

"So are you."

He shrugged out of his shirt, then stepped out of his pants. He'd worn a suit to the wedding. A crisp black suit with a stark white shirt. He'd been stunning. The most glorious sight she'd ever beheld.

She traced her bright red nails over his chest now, and almost moaned aloud as her body began to ache with a throbbing need for him.

"Are you ready?"

"Ready?" She asked guiltily, wondering if she'd spoken her needs out loud.

"To swim," he murmured, lifting her up and cradling her against his chest. This time, she resisted pointing out that he didn't need to carry her. Her heart was turning over with anticipation, but it had nothing to do with the idea of sinking into the warm, clear water.

"That too," he agreed with a slow-spreading smile, showing how perfectly he understood her.

He stepped into the pool, holding Sophie as though she were a feather. The water was deliciously warm against her skin, kept that way courtesy of the bright Mediterranean sunshine and its sheltered position from winds.

"Look at that view," she said with true wonderment.

"This view?" He teased, pointedly looking at her naked chest.

She blushed in a way that he found charming.

"You are my wife, *agape mou*, you do not need to be embarrassed when I compliment you."

"I know," she laughed. "You'd think I'd be used to it by now. But the truth is, and I know I can be honest with you now that you've signed me up for life, I've never, not in my whole life, been with someone like you."

He was careful not to betray a hint of emotion. "No?"

"Well, let's be realistic. It's not like guys like you are everywhere. You are a pretty rare specimen after all, Mr Petrides."

"Endangered?" He said lightly, and he felt an answering sense of danger piercing his gut.

"Definitely," she agreed. He lowered her into the water so that just her head bobbed above the surface. "I'm in heaven."

"It is not a bad way to spend an evening."

"Did you ever think, when you were living on the streets, that this would be your future?"

"What do you think?" He said quietly.

"It upsets you. When I ask you about that time in your life?"

"No." His smile was unconvincing. "It upsets me when anyone presumes I am not still that same person. That I'm not still capable of doing whatever it takes to get my way." He was joking, but his words sent a little frisson of emotion through her.

"I don't think that." She wrapped her arms around his waist and ignored that instinctive trickle of warning. "I think you're exactly the same person. I think that boy always had the potential to be what you are. That's what Pierre saw in you. The real you."

Damn her! The certainty that she was a siren filled him once more; she was able to use her beautiful voice and words to fill in the gaps in his soul and leave total contentment in their place.

"I see the real you," she kissed his shoulder; it was wet and his skin was warm. Her lashes fanned against her cheeks as she thought again what she'd said only moments earlier. She was in heaven. Having never felt lonely nor unhappy, she understood now that until meeting Alex, she'd been living a half-life. She hadn't realised it, but the ecstasy of their marriage was undeniable.

"Do you?" He asked with a hint of disbelief. For how could she? He had married her to get her out of his sister's life. He had seduced her to make her more his than she was Eric's. Did she truly believe she understood him? Even he couldn't quite believe how low he'd stooped.

Only by holding onto the belief that she deserved this was he able to quell his guilt. He was almost positive she'd been in an inappropriate relationship with Eric. There'd been no definitive smoking gun, but within the space of a week, he'd seen too many hushed conversations to be ignored. Not to mention that infuriating *tete a tete* he'd witnessed as Eric had emerged from her bedroom!

Those events, coupled with the fact she'd been involved with her previous employer amounted to one undeniable fact, in Alessandros's mind. His wife had made a habit of mixing business with pleasure, and this last time, she'd picked the wrong wife to wound.

"Of course." She lifted a hand to his cheek. Though he'd shaved that morning, before the wedding, it had grown back quickly, covering his square jaw with a prickly beard.

"And what do you see?"

"I see someone determined. Someone good. And someone kind." She blinked up at him and he could have groaned for how stunning she was in the soft moonlight.

She was a woman designed to tempt men.

Well, he had put a stop to that, at least so far as other, married men went. Men like his brother-in-law.

But at what cost?

Would he be able to resist her power? Or would he fall just as in love with her as the poor mugs before him?

"And I see the real you," he said, reminding himself as much as her that he knew what motivated her.

"I should hope so." She pushed away from him so that she could swim to the edge of the pool. She braced her arms across its coping and stared down at the ocean below.

Yes, he saw the real her. She was scheming, manipulative, sexy and irresistible.

He moved behind her, and braced himself on either side of the pool, an arm on either side of her head.

"Excuse me, sir." At the sound of Alena, Sophie startled.

"Relax. It is only my housekeeper," he whispered into her ear, keeping his body where it was to shield Sophie's nakedness from view.

"There is a phone call for Mrs Petrides."

"Who is it?" His voice was a bark.

"Mr Sandhurst, sir."

"Eric?" She said, and Alex imagined he felt the quiver of anticipation in her voice. His temper spiked.

"Tell him Mrs Petrides is otherwise occupied," he growled, more harshly than he'd intended.

"Alex," Sophie whispered, wishing to turn around but not wanting to risk exposing herself to anyone.

"Sophie, it is our wedding night. Unless there is something drastically wrong, Eric will not interrupt us."

"But the twins ..."

"Are fine."

"How do you know?" She demanded, her voice rising in intensity.

"Because. Helena would have called me if there was a problem."

"Then it must be something else. Something important." She thought of Helena, and a trickle of anxiety ran through her. "Please, Alex. I'll be quick."

He compressed his lips, his temper dark.

"Alena, please bring a phone to Mrs Petrides."

"Yes, sir."

The housekeeper walked back towards the house, and once she'd disappeared inside, Sophie turned in the water.

"I had no idea we weren't alone."

"We are alone."

"Um, there was just someone here."

"Alena and Harry are my domestics."

"And therefore they don't count?"

"Well," he smiled despite his contained fury. "Yes, they count. But they are used to being unseen, and to not seeing."

Sophie wondered at the impact of his words. Strangely, for she knew him to be a renowned womaniser, she hadn't really thought of him with other woman before then. Now?

"I guess I'm not the first woman you've brought here."

He felt a sense of satisfaction at her obvious hurt. It was beneath him, and yet he'd relished in inflicting the blow. "No."

She nodded slowly, her eyes not meeting his.

"As I don't doubt I'm not your first lover," he said slowly. Pryingly.

"No," she nodded. "You're not."

Hmm. Interestingly, the discomfort was not one-sided. He didn't like the way his gut clenched at her admission.

"You're my second."

Alessandros was very still. Even his eyes didn't move. She lies. She lies well. She is manipulative.

He didn't even want to dignify her assertion with a response. Thankfully, Alena appeared before it was required of him.

She held the cordless phone on a tray, and Alex marvelled at the gesture, as he always did. It made him feel a little like James Bond when his domestics did that kind of thing. As though he was truly lord and master with bonafide servants.

He took the phone and handed it to Sophie, but didn't swim away.

"Eric, hey," she said, her voice unmistakably upbeat.

Alex couldn't hear anything other than the muted hum of Eric's words; certainly not enough to discern the detail of what he was saying.

"I ... can't really talk about that now," she said, her eyes lifting to Alex.

"I understand. Just what we usually do. Yeah. Why don't I call you in the morning? You'll be fine. Eric? I have to go." A pause while Eric said something else. "Okay, yes. I know. I know. Me too. Okay. Bye."

She handed the phone back to Alex and he pressed the red button to disconnect the call. The time it took for him to pass the receiver back to Alena should have been enough to calm him, and yet he still felt a force of emotion in his gut when he turned to face his bride.

"I presume there was no disaster?" His voice, despite the torrent of feeling he was experiencing, was cynically cold.

"No." She bit down on her lip. Something had changed within his bride. She was worried. Or was she missing Eric? He closed his eyes briefly on a wave of regret.

This plan had seemed simple at first. But if he stopped and thought about it, nothing was simple about marrying a woman he really, really didn't trust. And deep down, possibly didn't even like.

Beyond sex, what did they have?

He lifted his hands to her hips and brought her towards him. When he kissed her, it was with the deliberate intention of wiping anything from her mind but him and that moment. Their silky bodies were wet beneath the water.

He discarded her flimsy underwear and took possession of her with a desperate hunger, made all the more desperate by a simmering anger. Against the edge of the pool, he made her his, and he made sure she understood. Eric – whatever he'd meant to her before – was in the past. He, and this odd marriage of theirs, was her future.

* * *

Sophie stretched her arms above her head. A week of marriage to Alessandros Petrides had defied every single one of her expectations.

Her body was relaxed and satisfied, and she seemed to be existing in a permanently exhausted state. Days were merging seamlessly into nights, as they seemed to go from bed, to the pool, then back to bed, occasionally pausing to eat a meal – just enough to sustain them and ensure their energy wouldn't wane.

Her smile was enigmatic as she let out a low noise of contentment.

Across the room, in the act of dressing fully for the first time since their wedding, Alex stilled. In the reflection of the floor to ceiling mirror, he caught his wife's image, and a tangle of dark emotions jostled within him.

He had married her to remove an impediment from his sister's life.

But making love to her had made her something else.

She was now an impediment in *his* life.

No. He returned to buttoning his shirt, his face scowling darkly. That wasn't the right word. She was an addiction and a curse.

He knew her intimately. He knew what she liked. What she craved. What made her giggle. What made her groan. He knew that she liked to fall asleep with her head on his chest, listening to the pounding of his heart. He knew that she liked to hum to herself when she showered, and that she was always slightly off key. He knew that she hated wearing make-up and loved not wearing a bra. He knew that she had a libido that matched his, and a curiosity for the sensual world they had been exploring together. He knew that she considered apples and toast to be a complete food pyramid, particularly when topped up with coffee. And he knew that she liked to keep her toenails painted pink.

"Why are you putting on clothes?" She asked, and the hint of betrayal in her tone brought a reluctant smile to his face.

He moved back towards the bed, his manner difficult for Sophie to decipher. "I have to go to Athens today."

"Athens," she asked, her big blue eyes wide as they startled to his.

He made a sound of assent, and sat on the edge of the bed. He cupped a hand over her head, stroking her soft, flowing hair.

"For how long?"

"Only the day, or I would have suggested you come with me." He flicked his shirtsleeve, squaring the black diamond cufflinks into place.

"Oh." She dropped her gaze, wondering at the sense of loneliness and dread that was already crinkling her contentment.

"Another time, *agape mou*."

"Sure. Yes. Of course."

"You will miss me?" He prompted, pressing a finger beneath her chin. He wondered then at his masochistic streak. He was floundering in his plan.

"Do you want me to miss you?"

"Yes." He needed space. He needed to remind himself why he had married her. And yes, she was intensely desirable but also, she was simply a means to an end.

"Believe me, I'll miss you." She smiled up at him, her forlorn bearing apparently evaporating. "And I hope you'll miss me, too."

He smiled at her and went to kiss her, but she put a finger on his lips. Her hands dropped to his belt and she unhooked the buckle then slid it from his pants. Alessandros wanted to maintain his schedule for the day, but curiosity held him still.

She undid his pants quickly, and freed his length from the confines of his boxer shorts. His fascination and desire leapt forward in equal measure.

She sat on his lap, easing herself onto his arousal while her arms wrapped around his waist and her mouth sought his. She was in complete control, taking him at her pace, and he allowed her the freedom to dictate their love-making. Her need for him was a heady aphrodisiac.

Her fingernails scratched through his shirt and his impatience grew. She moved slowly and sweetly, but he wanted more. He gripped her hips, and took control, moving her faster and firmer, until her face was pink and her voice was a fever pitch of longing.

They ascended the heavens together, an orgasm tore through them as one; they held each other tight, their bodies a mass of limbs and flesh. Sophie could have wept.

Her need for him was a bottomless well. No matter how often they came together, she craved him with a terrifying intensity.

"I will miss you." His voice was gravelly. His hands – so insistent when they were making love – were gentle now as they stroked her nakedness lovingly.

"Why are you going?" She shifted her weight, and he smiled as he felt her body flicker in a post-love-making reaction.

"I am interviewing your replacement."

"My replacement?" She startled, shifting her head so she could look at him properly.

"Mmm. Helena will need help, now that you are here with me."

"Oh!" She blinked, her features showing her surprise. "Surely that's something Eric and Helena should handle?"

She didn't understand the expression in his eyes. "My sister has entrusted me with the hiring of her aid."

Sophie chewed on her lower lip.

"You do not think this is a good idea?" He prompted, running his hands over her arms until he could link his fingers in hers.

"I ... no. I didn't say that."

"Yes, you did," he laughed. "You said it with the this little pout," he ran a finger over her lips. "And this little line," he pointed between her brows.

She nodded slowly. The secret worries she had about Helena had been becoming more and more burdensome. Not telling the man she loved that she thought Helena was suffering from depression now felt like a giant omission. The loyalty that had been so easy to claim for Eric was now being torn in two. Ultimately, she had to think of Helena and the boys. What was best for them? Helena needed help, of that Sophie was absolutely certain. And the boys?

Her heart squeezed painfully in her chest as she pictured them. A wave of sadness swept over her. The boys. Were they missing her as she was them?

She moved away from him, and stood, nibbling her lower lip as she tried to work out how to move forward. "It's important to find the right fit," she said quietly, toying with the silky blonde ends of her hair.

"Of course," he agreed, standing and redressing.

But Sophie was anxious. "Do you have long before you go?"

"I am already later than I intended to be, courtesy of my wife."

She swallowed past the anxiety in her throat. "I'll see you tonight?"

"I'll be late. Don't wait up." He kissed the tip of her nose and then stalked from the room. She watched him go with the certainty that she no longer knew who she was.

How had she let that happen?

She'd known him for barely a month! A month! And she could no longer see where she ended and he began.

She kept herself busy to stave off the way she missed him. Corfu was a beautiful island, and the town was a relatively short drive from Alessandros's villa. But she didn't yet feel up to driving one of his expensive sports cars, especially on the wrong side of the winding roads. And so she explored his villa instead. Rooms of beautiful things, it had been expertly decorated. There were photographs of Helena and the children in several of the rooms, and in the loft upstairs, a collection of pictures they'd posted to him over the years.

Sophie ate well. She had a whole week to make up for, and Alena seemed intent on spoiling her. The olives, cheese, tomato, baguette, cured meats and roast lamb seemed to stretch forever, but Sophie wasn't complaining.

It was a relief, though, when dusk fell over the island, casting a pale golden glow over the villa, which gradually gave way to darkness.

Sophie settled with her iPad and was about to email her sisters when the phone began to ring. It was late, and she didn't want Alena to be disturbed, and so she scrambled for the handset.

It was at that exact moment that Alex arrived back at the Villa. His day had been long, though fruitful. He had selected an excellent candidate for Helena. A woman with miles of experience, and a distinctly unglamorous bearing.

She would be of little interest to Eric; the children and Helena would be safe.

He reached for the phone instinctively, grabbing it just as the ringing stopped.

"It's me."

He froze in the hallway as he recognised Eric's voice instantly.

"Eric, is everything okay?"

"I suppose so." Alex grimaced. His old friend was grumbling like a child.

"What's the matter?"

"We miss you."

"I miss you, too. I was almost in tears today, thinking of those boys." Of course, missing the twins had only been a part of her sulking. Mainly, it had been her husband she'd been thinking of.

There was a long silence, heavy with Eric's worry.

"Eric, how's Helena?"

"That's what I'm calling you about."

"What is it?"

Something in Sophie's voice caught Alex's attention. She was worried. He gripped the handset tightly.

"Did you tell Alex anything?"

"No!" She sighed softly, and Alex could just picture her, the way her beautiful mouth would have swelled around the soft exhalation of breath.

"You mustn't. I've been thinking about it. He would never forgive me."

A dark emotion coursed through Alex.

"Eric …"

"I mean it, Sophie. It has to stay between you and me. At least until I've talked to Helena. Promise me."

"Eric …"

"Promise me!" Eric's tone was desperate.

"Eric, this is no one's fault."

Alex clenched a fist by his side. Is that seriously how his wife was justifying an affair with a married man.

"Alex would be furious. With both of us."

"Don't you think I know that?" She sighed again, but this time, it was loaded with angst. "I almost told him this morning, Eric."

"You did what? Sophie, don't be crazy! He'll shoot the messenger. If anyone's going to have this conversation with him, it's me."

"But I hate lying to him. I hate keeping it from him. Don't you think he deserves to know?"

"I think it will make an enormous, dramatic mess if you get him involved."

"He is involved! He's my husband. And Helena's brother."

"Yes, and he is my friend."

Sophie sobbed. "This is such a mess. We have to do what's right, Eric."

"Then just ... don't do or say anything yet. Not until I work out what to do about Helena." Eric made a frustrated sound. "This would be so much easier if we could meet in the kitchen for one of our late night sessions, wouldn't it?"

She smiled as she remembered their shared love of coffee and the midnight hours. "I'll try to get over to see you all soon." She thought of how lonely she'd been that day. "Perhaps next time Alex is travelling." She would do anything to avoid being alone in the house without him, rattling around like a lovesick teenager.

Alex disconnected the call silently and stood, staring at the white wall opposite.

Everything he had thought to be true had just been confirmed, and in the most treacherous manner! To hear his wife and Eric casually discussing the hushing up of their affair – or worse, the continuation of it – was sickening.

He spun on his heel and walked back out the front door of his home. He needed to cool off before he saw her, or he wasn't sure what he'd say. In that moment, he felt the angriest he'd ever been in his life.

"I'm sorry to bother you with this when you're a loved up newlywed."

She grimaced. "It's fine. I know how worried you are. I just wish there was more I could do to help. The thing is, I know Alex would want to know. I know he would be able to help ..."

"God, Soph. You're his wife, but I've known him for years. When it comes to Helena, he is just totally controlling. If he thought her to be unhappy, he'd make it worse."

"I just think you're being unfair. He's a great man. And he loves you both, not just Helena ..."

Eric sighed. "I know. Just ... let me try to get Helena on-board. Sometimes I think she realises how dire things are. Other times, she's in complete denial."

Sophie nodded. "Okay. I hear what you're saying. But there has to be a time limit on it. I can't keep this secret from the man I love for much longer."

"It's such a bloody mess. Helena just clams up whenever I mention it."

"I know." She nodded into her lonely bedroom. "We'll work it out."

She disconnected the call to Eric with no idea that her own life was the one in tatters; that Alex had overheard only part of the conversation and leaped to all the wrong conclusions.

CHAPTER FIVE

Three full days had passed with no word from Alex. Only a brief text message on his first night away to let her know he'd been held up. When she'd asked him when he expected to return to their home, he hadn't responded. Nor had he responded to her call the next day. Nor her call the day after that.

Sophie's loneliness and ache for him was now eating her alive. She sat at the kitchen table, staring unseeing at the ocean. How had she come to depend on him so completely in such a short period of time? Where was the strong, independent, world-travelling woman she'd prided herself on being? She was well aware that her moping was setting any kind of feminist movement back fifty years, and yet she was incapable of breaking the fog.

"I miss you." The simple three words sat blinking on her phone. She hovered her finger over the send button. It was far too insipid for how she felt. Her body, having never known the kind of pleasure Alessandros was capable of invoking, was now in agony for the deprivation of it.

She tapped back over the keys and tried again. "I am in agony without you."

Ugh! Far too needy. She dropped the phone to the table and focussed back on the ocean. It rolled in and out with a reassuring regularity. Sophie wondered distractedly what it felt like at that time of year? The days were still warm, though Autumn had officially begun and before long, a Christmas chill would settle over the continent. Even here in Greece, the seasons would shift.

Her phone buzzed and she scrambled for it with such haste that she sent her tea flying to the ground. She ignored the mess; it would wait. Her phone began to bleep, and she prayed, as she swished it open, that she would hear from her husband.

I will be home late tonight.

Sophie read the words with a strange feeling of confusion.

Where was the emotion? Where were the 'x's he had signed off with previously? At least, she thought with a small flicker of pleasure, he would be back. Then everything would feel normal. Then, it would be fine.

Feeling like even more of a traitor to womanhood in general, she quickly mopped up her tea and then set about preparing for him. Thoughts of dinner fled from her mind completely; instead, she thought only of Alex. She wandered the garden and collected wildflowers. Frangipani, hibiscus, and the spiky bougainvillea that grew rampant over one side of his villa, all pulled together to make a bright and fragranced arrangement. She set it on his side of the bed, and then bathed in the beautiful milk and honey lotion he'd given her as part of her wedding present. She shaved her legs and moisturised them until they were soft and silky, and styled her hair into a loose bun at her nape.

She wore only a simple black dress, low cut at the front and scooped at the back, it fell to her knees with a little kick, drawing attention to her slender form.

And then, she waited. Nine o'clock came and went. Ten o'clock followed. And then eleven. It was almost midnight when Alex finally returned. Perhaps he hadn't expected her to wait up for him, because he walked into the house silently. Sophie, from the armchair in the lounge, watched as he placed his keys on the sideboard and then ran a hand over his neck.

He looked ... wonderful. And yet tired, too. He'd undone his tie and it was loose around his neck. His shirt was unbuttoned to reveal a strong column of neck and some coarse hair, which she knew ran down the middle of his taut waist, into his pants. Sophie felt her body stir instantly at the thought of his nakedness.

He stood in the hallway for a very long time. Not moving, not doing anything, except thinking.

Had something happened? Was something the matter? She ached for him in a way that she hadn't known possible, and yet she stayed where she was. Though he was her husband, his absence had done something to her confidence. She no longer felt, as she had done only days earlier, as though she had a right to touch him.

As though he could feel her intent gaze, his eyes lifted quickly and landed on her with a sharp, searing inspection. And Sophie gasped. Her stomach was in knots; her heart was pounding into her ribs.

"Hi." It was a strangled whisper; a plea into the night air.

He walked towards her slowly. Sophie might have even said reluctantly. And when he was close enough, she breathed in deeply and let his intoxicating fragrance soothe her nerves. Only it didn't. Her body lurched with remembered sensations and she found herself standing on autopilot.

"Where have you been?" Her anguish was obvious in her voice. He ignored it.

"I told you. I was held up."

His words were spoken with unmistakable coldness. She tried to ignore it, but a sense of uncertainty was haunting her.

"Did you ... did you find a nanny?"

"A nanny?" He dragged his dark gaze over his wife. She looked better than he remembered and he loathed the way his body responded to her, with a shocking degree of awareness and need.

"For Eric and Helena?"

At the mention of her lover, something inside of Alex snapped. Sanity? Temper? He lifted his hands to the flimsy straps of her dress and slid them down her arms, without taking his eyes from her face.

"Yes."

"Oh, good. I'm glad. The boys are such a handful. They'll need help now that I'm here. With you." She was babbling. Her dress had fallen to the floor. She was completely naked before him and he was looking at her as though for the first time.

"I've missed you." She was begging him to say it back. To say something that would quell the pooling uncertainty that was filling her heart and mind.

"Let us see how much."

"What do you mean?"

His eyes stayed on hers, and there was a faintly mocking quality to them.

"I mean, my dear, beautiful wife, that I want to fuck you until you scream this house down. And then I want to fuck you again." His anger was a force riding high with his desire, and he enjoyed using the harsh language with her. "If you would be so kind as to undress me."

"I ..." Her eyes flashed briefly with the hurt that was in her heart but she told herself to ignore it. Hadn't she been craving him with a desperate hunger? Now he was home, and the first thing he wanted was to make love to her. Sure, she wanted more than sex, but for the moment, sex would at least answer one of her needs.

Her fingers trembled as she unbuttoned his shirt. He watched with growing impatience as she fumbled with the buttons and then slid it from his body. When she knelt to attend to his pants, he groaned in anticipation. She was slow, but it only added fuel to the fire of his need. He undressed with an economy of movement, then put his hands down to pull her to standing.

Only she stayed at knee level, her big eyes looking up at him. Her cheeks were flushed; she was eye-height with his arousal and it was confronting.

"I ... Alex ..."

"Yes, Sophie?"

Sophie told herself she must be wrong. He wasn't being condescending. He was ... being Alex. Bossy, controlling, domineering, impatient, wonderful Alex. "I've never, um, done this, but ..." Her blush deepened as her fingers wrapped hesitantly around his length. She moved her mouth forwards and tentatively she took his tip into her silky moistness. His body flinched in automatic response to the sweet contact. Instinctively, she ran her tongue around his tip and then took more of him in her mouth.

Alex groaned softly and his hands tangled in her hair, against her scalp, as she showed him that, whatever she claimed, she was either startlingly experienced or gifted with all forms of intercourse. He stepped backwards before he lost control altogether and masked his features with effort. "This is not the time to learn to ride a bike."

Sophie was confused. And hurt. That much was obvious in the way her features crumpled. He hated how much pleasure he took from that fact. It was beneath him. Or it should have been.

"Was it not ... I mean ... I'm sorry. I don't know what I'm doing."

She stood and turned away from him, her breathing ragged. The embarrassment was licking through her and Alex almost weakened. Only the memory of her treachery and dishonesty made it impossible for him to view her with anything other than contempt.

"I am not in the mood to be patient for release, Sophie. It has been three long days."

"Tell me about it," she snapped, spinning back to face him, her cheeks pink and her eyes shimmering with the threat of tears.

"I would rather show you," he said darkly, stalking towards her and linking his fingers through hers. He pulled her hand and then he kissed her with a dark intensity, his tongue almost punishing in her mouth. But she groaned and her leg lifted to curve around his back. He took advantage of her posture to slide a finger inside her warmth. She was so wet and ready for him that he moaned against her.

He didn't want to wait until they reached his bedroom. He wrapped his arms around her waist, holding her body to his, and pressed her back onto the lounge suite. When she was flat on her back, he stood and looked at her. She was so beautiful it hurt.

"Do you trust me?"

The question burned into her brain. Did she? In that moment, she was feeling a conflicting range of emotions. But she nodded, and licked her lower lip.

"Good." He cast about until his eyes landed on his belt. He bent to retrieve it and then wrapped it around her wrists, looping it through the leg of the marble occasional table that sat behind her.

"Alex?"

His smile was brief. "You will enjoy it."

"I just want to feel you."

"And you will. Eventually."

He stood back again to admire the view of his wife, tied and panting beneath him. Yes. He was going to pleasure her, and pleasure her again. He hovered his body over hers and ran his tongue from her lips, down her chin, to the cleft between her breasts. Her breathing was already rushed. When he began to lace his tongue lower, tracing invisible lines down past her belly button, to the hair-softened apex at the top of her thighs, she cried out and writhed.

She had almost driven him insane with the intimate kiss she'd given him. Now, it was his turn. His tongue ran between her folds, seeking her most intimate core. She bucked hard against him, her shock fierce.

He laughed against her and continued his invasion, using his fingers to give him access. Sophie was almost wild with pleasure. Arrows of heat and desire and need were barbing against her skin. She dug her heels into the sofa and cried out loudly, begging Alex. Begging him to take her. She ripped at her wrists but the leather of the belt against the weight of the marble held her perfectly imprisoned. He moved one hand up to her breasts and he squeezed a nipple until she felt stars in her eyes. The pleasure was the most magnificent thing she'd ever experienced. She needed more. She needed everything.

"Please, Alex, please. I'm begging you."

"Have you ever felt like this, my wife?"

"No," she shouted, not wondering why he'd ask such a question.

"Has anyone ever made you scream like this?"

"No."

"Do you want me?"

"Yes! Shit! Please!"

He laughed and then lifted his mouth higher, to her other breast. He took it in his mouth and brought his arousal tantalisingly close to her entrance. Sophie lifted her hips, trying desperately to take him in deep, to feel him inside her, but he kept moving out of her reach.

"Please," she whispered over and over, as her orgasm began to make her brain fog.

"Use my name,"

"Alex," she substituted, and now she said his name, over and over again.

"Say, *Alex, fuck me.*"

She blinked her eyes open, confusion breaking the spell for the briefest of moments. He moved just inside her, and then pulled back out again. His desertion made her moan.

"Say it."

"Please fuck me."

"Alex, fuck me," he corrected.

"Alex, fuck me," she repeated through gritted teeth. She pulled at her wrists, a dark emotion combining with her total, rampant need for him.

"Yes," he muttered. "Good girl."

He drove his length into her hard, so that her breasts wobbled and her body shuddered. She cried out in relief as finally she felt his whole length in her body.

"More, please."

"Alex, fuck me," he reminded her.

"I don't understand."

"This is what I want you to say to me, from now on."

"But ..."

He pulled out of her, his dark eyes glinting as he stared stubbornly at his wife. His own desire was obvious. His cheeks were dark beneath his tan and his arousal was rock hard. And yet he stayed away from her as though it were as easy for him as anything in the world.

"Alex, fuck me," she mumbled, too torn up by her desire to refuse. A time would come to untangle the damage his words had caused. But it was not then.

He thrust into her once more, hard and Sophie cried out as she felt an orgasm bursting upon her soul. It was fierce and hot, and it made her whole body convulse. Alex waited until her breathing slowed, and then he reached forward and unhooked the belt.

With a monumental effort, he pulled away from his wife and stood. He didn't look at her as he walked across the room and scooped up his clothes. He pulled his shorts on, but it was agony to do so. The fabric against his sensitive arousal made him want to take her back in his arms until he exploded.

But he wouldn't give her the satisfaction of seeing that he was just as crazy for her as she was for him. Hurt at her duplicity was a force that he found easier to process as rage; betrayal was better expressed as cold resentment.

Sophie sat up and rubbed her wrists. They were pink from the belt. Her insides were quivering and now, satiated by the release of such a tremendous orgasm, she sat in stone-cold shock.

What the hell had just happened?

"Alex ..."

He was buttoning up his shirt, his back to her. His pants followed suit. Then, patiently, his face calm and certainly without emotion, he turned to face her. "Yes?"

Sophie hadn't realised she was crying until a tear splashed down onto her naked thigh.

"I can't believe that just happened."

"Oh?" He arched a dark brow. "You did not want it?"

"I ... I wanted you ..."

"And you got me," he shrugged insolently. "Is there any food?"

"Food?" She felt a bubble of rage in her chest. "What the hell? Don't you think you owe me an apology?" She stood her voice shaking and her body trembling. But now, it was from fury, not lust.

"For what, Sophie?" He asked wearily, as though she were boring him. "For fucking you as you kept demanding me to do?"

"Don't!" She stormed over to him, her body tense. "You made me say that. I wanted my husband to make love to me. I wanted you. I've missed you." Her heart was twisting painfully in her chest. "I wanted you. I love you," she whispered, her words haunted.

"And I love fucking you," he said with a drawl. "Food?"

Sophie stared at him, her mind shuffling in a strange way. Everything he'd ever said. Everything he'd promised her. Why had he married her?

Her blue eyes examined him for a long time, trying to find some semblance of the man she knew. But in his place was this hard-hearted, rude megalomaniac.

"Go to hell," she said finally and stormed away from him. Only where could she go? Not to their room, with its beautiful flower arrangements and the scent of hope and passion in the air. She went up another level, and selected a guest room at random. Two of the towelling robes that hung in each room were against the door. She wrapped one around her shaking frame and went to lie down. Only a moment later, nausea and shock combined in her gut and she had to bolt to the ensuite. She vomited until there was nothing left in her stomach and then she crawled back to bed, hot, cold, shocked and miserable.

What had happened to her husband?

And what was she going to do?

* * *

All night, he lay awake, staring at the ceiling. Flashes of memory scorched his brain, and kept him from sleeping.

He had decided, whilst in Athens, that he hated his wife. That he hated her for what she'd done to his sister, and what she obviously intended to continue doing to her. He hated her, and he had wanted to hurt her, perhaps in the same way Sophie had hurt Helena.

And yet it had made him feel ill to treat her with such contempt and disrespect. She might not deserve any better, and yet it sat like a knife in his gut that he'd behaved in such a fashion. He rolled over and stared at her empty side of the bed. It smelled like her. Sweet and soft.

He groaned and squeezed his eyes shut, but that was worse. Then he saw her face. The depth of emotion she was able to convey with one look was almost too much to bear. The betrayal and bewilderment might as well have been spelled out for him.

He rolled the other way, but his eyes landed on the stunning arrangement of flowers she'd put beside the bed. He imagined her forming this collection of wildflowers into a bouquet. She would have hummed as she did it, in her slightly off-key voice. Her hands would have moved deftly, as she created this sculpture in the vase. Bright, fragrant and spiked, they were, in many ways, symbolic of his wife's traits.

Then just ... don't do or say anything yet. Not until I work out what to do about Helena. This would be so much easier if we could meet in the kitchen for one of our late night sessions, wouldn't it?

Alex thwomped his fist into his pillow.

I'll try to get over and see you all soon. Perhaps when Alex is travelling next.

She hadn't gone to him, though. Alex had checked in with Alena every day, and made enquiries of his wife. When Alena had offered to get Mrs Petrides, Alex had employed his most indulgent tone and insisted that she not be disturbed.

But, nonetheless, his wife was evidently planning to continue the affair.

That, and only that, was what he needed to hold onto.

He stood with a sound of frustration, giving up altogether on the idea of sleep. He began to walk towards the door and then thought better of it. He retraced his steps angrily and lifted the vase of flowers. One of the bougainvillea stalks grazed his forearm with a sharp needle. Blood seeped out slowly.

He ground his teeth together as he carried the flowers out of the villa and dumped them in the garden beside the front door.

It was a cathartic act, and afterwards, he made a pot of coffee and settled to his desk. Work, the act of concentrating on problems he could easily solve, always calmed him.

And so he worked, hoping that eventually, calmness would come.

CHAPTER SIX

Hunger, finally, drove her from the guest room. Still wrapped in the robe, with a face that was ashen and eyes that were red, she padded downstairs slowly and silently. Perhaps, if she was very lucky, her husband would be gone.

She did not wish to – and felt she could not – face him yet.

Her luck, though, had deserted her. Alex was in the kitchen, dressed casually, staring out of the window at the rolling ocean. Sophie froze in the doorway, and began to step backwards.

Hungry or not, she couldn't do it.

Only he heard her and spun around, his face a dark mask of feeling before he smoothed it away. Sophie's throat worked overtime as she tried to bring moisture back to her mouth. Her traitorous body frothed with desire. She dropped her eyes away and moved to the opposite side of the kitchen. It was large; she could avoid him, even while being in the same room.

"Sophie." She stared at the kitchen bench as though it were suddenly the most fascinating thing she'd ever seen.

"Sophie," his word was a haunting reminder of how things had once been for them.

She swallowed but her throat was lined with razors. Nothing brought relief from the pain.

And what could he say, anyway? She bit down on her lower lip and shook her head slowly. "I just came down to get something to eat," her words were a husk. She cleared her throat and tried again. "I can't talk to you yet. I don't know what to say."

He was right behind her. She felt him before he spoke. He put his hands lightly on her shoulders and that now-familiar frisson of need began to bubble in her gut.

She couldn't tell if she turned to face him with reluctance or anticipation, only that she did spin in his arms. His face, at least, reflected some of her trepidation. He scanned her features with slow, deliberate curiosity and then wrapped his hands around her wrists. He lifted them and subjected them to the same steady study.

"Did I hurt you?"

Yes, she wanted to shout. Her heart had been smashed into a billion tiny pieces. But she knew that wasn't what he meant. She dropped her eyes and shook her head. The truth was, she'd never been more intensely satisfied than that night, and that terrified her.

"Sophie," it was a plea, torn from his body.

She lifted her eyes to his face again, uncertainty making her slow to speak.

"Are you looking for me to say that it doesn't matter? Or to somehow absolve you for what happened last night?"

He closed his eyes briefly. "No."

"Good." She pulled her wrists away and turned her back to him. She was starving, but the idea of staying in the kitchen was anathema to her. She pulled a banana from the fruit bowl and side-stepped away from him. "I don't know what happened, and I have nothing I can say to you right now."

He watched her move towards the door, and the words he'd been thinking all night were locked in his mind. *I was angry because you are cheating on me. Because you and Eric are involved and Helena and I deserve better.* But he couldn't say them. Pride and resentment held him quiet.

And so, when she was almost out of the kitchen he said instead, "I am leaving again today."

Only the fact that she stopped walking showed that Sophie had heard him. She nodded without turning back. "Okay." He suspected tears had softened the word. He swore softly under his breath and dragged a hand through his hair. She was taking the piece of fruit and walking out of the villa, toward the terrace that overlooked the sea. Too late he thought of the flowers he'd discarded in the middle of the night.

They were there, and of course she saw them. The flowers lay in scattered disarray by the door. From the shade of the decked area, her eyes kept drifting to them. They were a perfect symbol of the strangely broken state they found themselves in. A graphic representation of her dashed hopes and ridiculous-seeming enthusiasm.

But was it so ridiculous? Married for a week, and separated for nights, she had missed him with an entirely appropriate intensity. They had parted with warmth; they had married out of love. So what had happened?

The more Sophie thought about it, the more she realised that she was missing something incredibly important. People didn't just switch their emotions like that. It wasn't possible.

She thought back to all the beautiful memories she had of their early acquaintance and a smile touched her lips. He did love her. Their marriage was founded on the kind of heart-scoring intensity that made it brightly real and overpowering.

The hateful flowers were mocking her. She moved further from the house, down the steep side garden that led to the ocean. A large rock was beneath a tree; she sat on it so that she could brood in comfort.

For Alex to have reverberated with such cold anger the night before must surely have meant that something had happened.

But what?

For the life of her, Sophie couldn't imagine ... until she could. Realisation dawned with the most sublimely perfect clarity that she startled.

He knew about Helena.

She dropped her head forward and gasped.

He knew about Helena, and what was more, she'd bet her last penny that he knew she and Eric had kept it from him.

Sophie stood abruptly and walked quickly back towards the house.

"Alex?" She almost ran down the hallway, and with each step she took, she became more and more convinced that she was right.

"Alex?" She stood very still and waited to hear noise. But the house was silent. Only Alena, out washing the walls near the pool, was moving in the midst of apparent calm. Sophie moved to her on autopilot. "Excuse me, Alena, have you seen Mr Petrides."

"No, I'm sorry, ma'am," she responded in broken English.

"Damn it." She spun around and planted her hands on the hips. She surveyed the house from between shuttered eyes.

Had he already left? She moved back into the house and checked the bedroom they'd shared. The bed was made. Her eyes were drawn to his empty bedside table and she thought again of the beautiful arrangement she'd left there. The gift he'd discarded.

Because he had been upset! Angry! Hurt!

Yes!

He had discovered something whilst interviewing the nanny. Perhaps he'd spoken to Helena, or Eric. Something had happened; it was as clear to her as the diamond she wore on her ring finger.

She ran upstairs again, into the room she'd used the night before and lifted her phone. A little red number called her attention to her messages and she opened them, her heart in her throat with the hope that she'd find Alex had already messaged to explain.

But it wasn't Alex. It was a number she didn't recognise.

"I'm here! Only I don't know where in Corfu you are. Send me the address."

She frowned, and was about to delete it without replying when the same number began to show on her screen as a call. Impatient, she answered with a gruff, "Yes?"

"Well, that's no way to greet your sister."

Sophie felt tears spring to her eyes at the welcome sound of Olivia's voice.

"You're here? In Greece?"

"I'm in Kerkyra. I found a bar not too far from the airport. This place is amazing. I could get lost in ancient laneways very happily."

Sophie thought despondently of the exploration she hadn't done. The island had been beckoning, and she'd been too wrapped up first in Alex, and then in desolation, to do any of it justice.

"I'll come to you," she decided instantly. "Only I've got no idea how the hell to get to the town, so you'd better make yourself comfortable."

"Can't my new brother-in-law drive you?"

"Alex?" Sophie's heartbeat accelerated. "He could, but he's ... away working."

"Already? Some honeymoon."

Sophie's cheeks flushed. "He's busy, Liv."

"I know, I know. The price you pay for marrying a tycoon, ha?"

"Yeah, I guess so." She dug her toe into the carpet.

"Well? Hurry up. I'll order you a champagne."

"Oh... I'll be driving ..."

"Pish. Hurry up. I miss you!"

Sophie laughed. "Why didn't you tell me you were coming? I would have arranged everything."

She could practically hear Liv's careless shrug. "I got a deal on a last minute flight. I hope it's okay?"

"Okay. It's bloody fantastic. I'll see you soon."

She moved quickly back to the bedroom and pulled a colourful dress off a hanger. It was a gorgeous shade of peach and turquoise and flattered her skin tones and eyes. The dress was simple cotton, strapless so that it ran straight across the top of her cleavage, hugged her to the waist and then flared in a short skirt to inches above her knees. It was perfect for the warm weather they'd been enjoying. Sophie slipped a pair of wedge-heeled sandals onto her feet and tidied her hair, then moved through the house.

The problem, of course, was that she had no idea where the cars were, and nor did she know who kept the keys. "Alena?" She emerged almost apologetically back to the pool.

"Yes, ma'am?"

"Please, call me Sophie." She said with a smile. "My sister has come to the island, and I'd like to go and collect her. Only I've no clue where the garage is."

"Ah!" Alena's face broke out into the most genuine smile Sophie had seen her employ since coming to the island. "That eez wonderful. But 'Arry will drive you."

"No, no, I don't want to disturb him."

"Mr Petrides 'as asked 'im to 'elp you."

"Oh." She nodded awkwardly. "If it's no trouble then."

Sophie hadn't yet met Alena's husband but she knew he busied himself in the gardens and with the fleet of vehicles Alex kept on Corfu. When Alena appeared with him a few moments later, Sophie saw he was a short, round man with a twinkling gaze and kindly expression.

"It's an honour," he said, in native English.

"Likewise."

"Alena says you would like to go to town?"

"Yes," she nodded. "To Kerkyra. My sister's there," she finished lamely.

"My wife said. Are you ready?"

"Now? Yes. Yes I am." She was suddenly desperate to see Olivia. Her sister could surely make everything seem better.

"Then let's go."

Sophie fell into step beside him as he made his way along the courtyard towards a long, low barn. He pressed a button in his pocket and the gate slid open to reveal seven sports cars. Sophie counted them to be certain. They were each immaculate and prestigious. There were several with unpronounceable names she'd never even heard of.

He caught her looking at the row of cars and grinned. "Do you have a preference?"

She shook her head quickly.

"We'll take the Alfa. You'll like it. Fast and elegant." He opened the front passenger door for her. "It is one of Mr Petrides's favourites."

"Great." She swallowed back the painful discomfort at the reference to her husband. "You're from England?"

"Sure am, ma'am. Up north way."

"Please, please, I beg you, stop calling me ma'am." She already felt like a weird imposter. The confidence that she belonged in Alex's life and home had rapidly evaporated.

"Mr Petrides prefers a degree of formality ..."

"Perhaps he does, but I can assure you, I don't." The engine purred to life and Harry steered it down the narrow drive with admirable expertise. "I'm Sophie. I'm Australian. We're not at all formal, really."

"Very well, ma'am."

She burst out laughing. It was hopeless. Better to accept her lot in life now that she was married to the all-powerful Alessandros Petrides.

"How far is town?"

"Under an hour."

"So far. I hadn't realised." She pulled her phone out and texted her sister. "I'm an hour away. Sit tight."

"Can't wait to see you!!"

Sophie shook her head with a fond smile.

The road from Alex's villa was so narrow that even the Alfa brushed the verge at times. It was right on the edge of a cliff, too, and beneath them, the ocean sparkled like diamonds dancing on liquid. Sophie was not nervous. Harry drove the car beautifully; he was confident and yet cautious, allowing her the freedom to simply enjoy the scenery. Much of the drive was through the less built up parts of the island. However, as they travelled further, eventually valleys and coves gave way to houses and shops. Before Sophie knew it, they were in downtown traffic, with the stunning laneways Olivia had referred to branching out in every direction.

"Oh!" She caught her breath as Harry turned a corner and the whole city opened up beneath them, like a blanket of terracotta rooves and sand-coloured walls. The buildings were straight-walled and flat-rooves, and they were built so close together that the car had to slow down to turn some corners. Shops with dark green awnings and gorgeous topiaried trees lined the sides of the road, and fountains cropped up as if from nowhere.

"This is stunning."

"Yes. We think so. Alena and I live in the old-town."

"Does it get older than this?" She queried with a tilt of her head.

He nodded. "The locals would call this the new part of town." She sent him a disbelieving look and he laughed. "It's only middle-aged. Where we live dates back to around twelve hundred BC. Not many of those buildings survive, of course, but the streets take a similar layout."

"That's absolutely mind-blowing."

"Where is your sister?"

"Ummm..." She checked her phone and then placed it in the console. "The Farfalla bar?"

He lifted his brows. "She has expensive taste."

Sophie laughed. "She has impeccable taste. More often than not, it tends to be expensive too, yes. Why? Is it a good place to go?"

"It is one of the premiere establishments on the island. Another favourite of your husband's."

Sophie nodded, but the little shards of jealousy were impossible to ignore. One didn't go to bars solo, after all. No doubt Alex had frequented this 'impeccable' establishment with his past lovers.

She swallowed the unpalatable thought. She was about to see Liv for the first time in almost a year. That, and only that, required her attention.

"Oh." She looked down at her dress with a grimace. "Will I be dressed ... I mean ..." her cheeks took on a becoming shade of pink and Harry found himself warming to his boss's wife. "Is there a dress-code?" She finished her question, smiling apologetically at the man.

"Believe me, ma'am, no one will turn away Mrs Petrides. You could go in there wearing little more than a rag and you'd still get the best table in the place."

Though he'd answered her question, his words were far from reassuring. Sophie caught her reflection in a tinted window as she moved towards the bar. Patrons were sitting at tables on the footpath in the very European al fresco style and there were little vases of bright purple flowers in the centre of each. Sophie moved past the other diners and towards the large glass and timber doors. They were opened inwards as she approached.

"Good afternoon," the man greeted in Greek.

Sophie checked her wrist watch and was surprised to see it was almost one o'clock. She scanned the restaurant and almost immediately saw her. Olivia Henderson, with her shimmering white-blonde hair, dark golden tan and sparkling green eyes, stood out anywhere. Here, in the midst of this glamorous bar, she looked like she'd walked off a catwalk, rather than a long-haul flight. And, unsurprisingly, she'd gathered a small crowd of admirers in the short time she'd been left waiting.

Sophie shook her head with a sense of amusement, and cut through the crowds.

"Hey!" Liv cried, cutting off one of the young men who was mid-sentence. "There you are!" She was taller than Sophie, and curvier too – with the kind of cleavage that was so generous it was almost an impediment. Or so Liv had complained on numerous occasions, when she'd found her dates so transfixed by her breasts that they were incapable of looking anywhere else for the duration of the meal. "Oh, my, God. I have missed you!" She wrapped her arms around Sophie's neck and held her tight.

Sophie sobbed into her sister's shoulder and nodded. The words she wanted to say were heavy in her mouth.

Liv pulled away, tears sparkling in her own eyes, as she lifted a hand to Sophie's cheek. "God, you look great. You look so polished!" She lifted Sophie's hand and made a low-whistle as she inspected the engagement ring Alex had surprised her with.

"That's got to be six or seven carats, right?"

Sophie nodded vaguely. Actually, it was nine carats, something which had seemed ludicrous and excessive but on which Alex had been insistent. The solitaire was so large that the platinum and diamond band that encircled it had needed to be weighted at the base, to stop it from constantly swirling around her slim finger.

"Wow. Okay. Drinks are on you," Liv teased, ignoring the group who'd been chatting to her and shepherding Sophie to a more private table by the window.

"Aren't you going to say goodbye to your new friends?"

She waved a hand impatiently through the air. "They were just fillers until you got here."

Sophie laughed affectionately. Olivia had always been the social butterfly of every room she entered. She'd made friends effortlessly and won hearts with almost as little trouble. She was charming and interesting, and generally, people forgave her everything.

A waiter appeared the moment they sat down. "Good afternoon," he greeted in slightly accented English. "Welcome to *Farfalla*. Have you been here before?"

No, but my husband has, Sophie swallowed the pithy remark and shook her head instead.

Olivia eyed her sister, and the worry that something was wrong was like a bullet in her chest. "We'd like to start a tab. And to be interrupted as little as possible." She reached into her bag and pulled out a card but Sophie shook her head.

"You've come all this way. Allow me." She hadn't yet used one of the credit cards Alex had given her. She slipped one from her wallet and handed it over, a little self-conscious when she realised it was one of those ridiculous Centurion Amex cards.

The waiter took it, examined it, and handed it back. "That will not be necessary, Mrs Petrides. Mr Petrides maintains an account here. Are you celebrating? Would you like some champagne?"

Sophie's cheeks were pink. She nodded helplessly and the waiter disappeared without pausing to confirm which label they'd prefer. When he returned, it was with the aid of another waiter, who ostentatiously held two champagne saucers while the first waiter peeled the top off the bottle. He popped it into a white-gloved hand and then handed the cork to Sophie. "It is to be kept. For luck and good memories."

"Oh." She slipped it into her bag with, perhaps, far less ceremony than was due, and then watched as the original waiter poured the champagne into first one glass and then the next.

"I shall keep the bottle in the fridge."

"Leave the bottle," Liv corrected. "We don't want to be interrupted unless our bottle is empty. Thank you."

Sophie shot her sister a warning glance, but the twitching of her lips spoiled the effect somewhat.

"What is this champagne?" Sophie whispered, once they'd left.

"Expensive, is what it is. At least two thousand dollars, I'd say."

Sophie spat out the bubbles she'd been sipping and clasped a hand over her mouth. "Oh my God! Livvie! You're not serious?"

Olivia shrugged. "A man bought one for me once, and that's what he said. It was the same label. I remember, because I'd never heard of it before that."

"Oh, Liv. We can't drink this."

Olivia's smile was deliciously cheeky. "Nonsense. It's been opened. Besides, they brought it over so naturally that one can only presume it's what your husbands makes a habit of drinking."

Sophie nodded. Olivia had a point. And again, she contemplated the unlikeliness of Alex drinking a bottle such as this on his own. No. It was what he shared with dates. Before he shared anything else with them. Like his home. And his body.

She flickered her gaze down to the table in a gesture designed to shield her thoughts from her sister, but Olivia knew Sophie far too well for that.

"How's married life?" She queried with an intentionally bland tone to her voice.

Sophie nodded. "It's good." She smiled anxiously. "It's just … an adjustment."

Olivia nodded. That could be it. "In what way?" She prompted, sipping her champagne and eyeing her sister over the rim of the glass.

"You saw what just happened right?" She shook her head slowly. "I've gone from barely making ends meet on a dreadful salary in London to being brought two thousand dollar bottles of champagne and being told my Goddamned Amex card isn't required here, at what my driver tells me is the most expensive bar in town." She rolled her eyes. "You know how weird this is."

Liv grinned. "I think I could get used to it pretty quickly."

Sophie burst out laughing. "Yeah, you probably could." She sobered. "You wait until you see his house. It's like this stunning, architectural, perfect palace. And when I say perfect, I mean … magazine perfect. Like Vogue Living ready *all the time*. It's … just … so much."

"But honey, you knew when you married him that he had this kind of money. What's the problem?"

"It's not a problem," she demurred quickly. "I love Alex." And she really, really did. No matter what was going on between them, she had every faith it would be a temporary concern. "It's just ... I fell in love with him when I didn't really have any concept of just how ..."

"Nonsense! Everyone knows how wealthy Alessandros Petrides is."

"Yes, yes. But you read a number in an article and that's very different to living it. Look at my engagement ring."

"I did, believe me," Olivia teased.

"I mean, I can't even imagine how much he spent on it. It's like ... all this is so normal to him. And I don't want it! I certainly don't need it."

"Then don't wear the ring. Buy yourself something simple and use that instead."

"But this is special because he gave it to me," Sophie pointed out with a shrug. "It's fine. I'm being silly. It's just an adjustment."

"Mmmm. You said that." Olivia pursed her lips in the style that was uniquely hers. "I like your hair like this."

Sophie might have laughed at the lightning fast conversation change, but she was used to her sister. "It's the same as always."

"No, it's longer, and blonder."

"Oh." Sophie shrugged. "The length is laziness, and the blonde must just be from the sun."

"It suits you. You look good."

Sophie's smile felt almost completely natural. "Thanks. So, are you going to tell me what adventure you're off on this time?"

Olivia leaned forward, her eyes glinting with excitement. "Vegas."

"I know where you're going, but not why."

"Why?" She scrunched up her nose as though Sophie was asking the most ludicrously simple question in the world. "Because it's Vegas."

"But what's in Vegas?"

"Bright lights. Action. Fun."

"You only got back from Rome a few months ago. Aren't you a little sick of all that?"

"Says the girl who married a hot, billionaire stallion about three seconds after meeting him. To say nothing of your decision to up and move to his palatial home in stunning Greece."

"We haven't moved here," Sophie corrected quickly, her tone distracted. "We're just ... staying here for now."

"You're missing my point! Your life is all about adventure! You were the first one to leave Celli. You escaped to Sydney as soon as you could and look at what you've done since. You've travelled with the bloody prime minister of England!"

"I might have been the first to leave home, but you're definitely making up for lost time." Sophie crossed one leg over the other with unconscious elegance.

"I know." Olivia shrugged. "You know me. I get itchy feet if I sit still for too long."

"What will you do for work?"

"I'll find something. Or something will find me." She grinned. "I have a friend who said they're looking for someone like me."

"You're so like mum sometimes, Liv," Sophie said with a shake of her head.

They were quiet for a moment, thinking of Meredith Henderson, a woman they'd loved so dearly, and had lost so tragically.

"Can you believe Cristiano's going to be back in the valley?"

"No," Olivia responded with a steady shake of her head. Her lips tugged downwards in one corner.

"What is it?" Sophie prompted, sipping her champagne and trying not to wonder how much that tiny amount of alcohol would have cost.

"It's just ... I don't think Ava's seeing the whole picture here. Cristiano's not the kind of guy to take news of a secret child lying down. He's going to be livid."

"Maybe, maybe not. Maybe he won't even find out," Sophie pointed out hopefully.

"They're staying at the vineyard. Milly's bound to make an impression on them."

Sophie couldn't help the smile that touched her expression. "Maybe. God, I miss that kid."

"I know, tell me about it." She ran a finger around the rim of her glass. "What are you worried about though? You know Cristiano's got no interest in kids. He's the proverbial bachelor. That was part of the problem."

"Look who's talking. You've gone and tamed one of those, so don't take it for granted that leopards can't change their spots."

"I haven't tamed Alessandro," Sophie demurred.

"He's a renowned ... well ... you know as much as I do, I presume. And you've got him stitched up and loved up."

"But Alex is nothing like Cristiano."

"Isn't he?" Olivia pushed.

"No." Sophie insisted. She drank her remaining champagne simply to break the conversation and Olivia topped their glasses up to stave off the reappearance of the over-attentive wait staff. "Cristiano's a bastard. He broke Ava's heart and left her pregnant and alone. Alex would never act like that. Ever. Family is hugely important to him."

"Yes, but Cristiano doesn't know he's got family in Australia, remember."

"That's not Ava's fault. She tried to tell him. He wouldn't see her. You can't possibly be defending him?"

"God, no." Liv shook her head. "I went with her to Rio, remember. I'll never forget the sight of our pregnant sister waddling away from his apartment building, having been turned away by his housekeeper." Sophie's eyes had a faraway expression. "And we both know what state she was in afterwards."

They didn't need to cover that in any more detail. The recollection of those dark days in Ava's life haunted them all. Thankfully, the sisters were so close-knit that they'd been able to pull together and help her through the post-natal depression and other complications. Between their support and the proper medical attention, Ava had come through the other side and returned to her normal self.

And Helena? Would her brother be able to help her in that unique way siblings had? Sophie leaned back into the leather seat, and focussed on one of the ornate lamps in the corner. Was she denying him the opportunity to help Helena, in a way that he'd never be able to forgive?

"Would you have told him?" Olivia wondered thoughtfully, conjuring out of nowhere an image of Cristiano's handsome, dark face.

"Absolutely," Sophie insisted. "He's the father. He should, if nothing else, have had the chance to support his child."

"Ava's doing okay in that department," Olivia pointed out.

"Yes, but Cristiano is a proud man. He would hate to know how she's been struggling, and how hard she's been working."

"I don't think he'd care." Liv shook her head. "Bastard."

"Yeah." It was a concise ending to the conversation. However, it was not the last conversation they would have on the matter. For that afternoon though, they filed it away for later prodding, and turned to more pleasurable matters. Hours passed in the blink of an eye, and before Sophie knew it, she was pleasantly fuzzy around the edges from excellent champagne, and her sprits were high courtesy of her funny, spontaneous sister.

"Okay, Mrs Petrides, I think it's time you took me to meet this sexy husband of yours."

Sophie felt her heart pound sharply in her chest. Alex. And just like that, her state of relaxation evaporated, to be replaced by one of anxious uncertainty. But what could she do? Her sister was in Greece, and of course she must meet the man who had swept Sophie off her feet. Even if they were barely speaking.

CHAPTER SEVEN

"Does he always work so much?" Olivia queried, stretching her legs to catch more of the sun.

"Yes," Sophie murmured, not opening her eyes for fear of the expression she might see reflected back at her.

"I've been here four days and am yet to see him."

"I'm aware of that," Sophie's words were sharper than she'd intended. She softened them with an apologetic smile. If she didn't take care, Olivia would start to worry that something was wrong. "I'm sorry. I miss him. Our wedding caught him as much off guard as it did me. He can hardly put his projects aside just to wait on us hand and foot."

"I'm not expecting him to. I only want to meet him before I go."

"You will. You don't have firm plans, I thought?"

"Itchy feet, remember?" She teased. "Besides, when he does get back, I don't want to cramp your style. Having seen how little you two get to see of one another, I don't want to be the annoying third wheel."

Sophie reached her hand out and curled it over her sister's. The water lapped in the pool at their feet, making a rhythmic sound that was quite soporific. "I'm glad you're here, Liv. I feel like we haven't just hung out like this in such a long time."

"I know. It's been far too long."

Alex paused at the edge of the paved area that led to the pool. His eyes briefly took in Olivia, and then slammed into Sophie. His gut twisted uncomfortably and acid formed in his throat. Her toes were pink, her skin tanned, and her hair silky. Even at this distance, he could catch a light hint of her sweet, vanilla fragrance, blowing to him on the afternoon breeze.

"It could only be better if Ava was here," Olivia murmured, stretched on a small sigh, and then turned around to reach for the sunblock. Only she saw the man who was on the edges of the pool deck and she smiled. "You must be Alex." She stood quickly and walked over to him, curiosity an actual force in her body.

"And with those eyes, I have no doubt you are my wife's sister."

His voice sent tremors of desire spiking through Sophie's blood. She felt her veins pounding with heat, and her throat was parched. But outwardly, she tried her hardest to stay calm.

"Olivia Henderson. Please, call me Liv."

"Liv," he agreed, shaking her hand. "I must apologise for my rudeness. I had an urgent matter in New York I had to attend to."

"New York." She spun to Sophie. "You never said he was in New York."

Sophie's bitterness was profound. She hadn't known. Alex hadn't told her. "No, I didn't." She responded casually, as though her husband's location didn't matter to her one bit. She couldn't put off greeting him any longer, but she wished fervently that her sister wasn't there, acting as a curious audience. She stood reluctantly, and began to make her way towards him. Every step made her heart race faster. She was in love with him, but she was also as mad as hell. Her eyes clashed with his, and her pulse fired loudly.

"Mrs Petrides," he murmured, moving towards her with his long stride, to close the distance. His expression was impossible to interpret. He lifted a hand to cup her cheek and lowered his head. His kiss was slow and it was desperate at the same time. Sophie felt her whole body electrify as though she'd been shocked, and she lifted her hands and tangled them in his dark hair. How easy it was to forget anything except Alex when he kissed her like that.

He pulled away from her but moved his mouth to her ear. His words were barely a whisper. "Kiss me like that and

I will take you right here on deck, with no care for who might be watching."

Colour darkened her cheeks and she stepped away from him as though stung. Olivia, watching the interaction with unashamed curiosity, arched a brow at her sister. "I was thinking of going for a walk. Alex, perhaps you could point me in the direction of the best paths."

"I can take you, honey," Sophie said quickly, her body and her mind all over the place. He was back. But she was still so angry with him. And yet she needed to speak to him. Her mind was firing like a cannon.

"No," Olivia shook her head. "I have a few calls to make."

"Then you can use Alex's study."

"No," Olivia laughed. She lifted her gaze to Alex and winked. "I think I should make myself scarce for a while." She scooped her book up from the lounger and lifted a hand in farewell. "I'll see you for dinner."

"Livvie," Sophie called after her retreating back, but Liv only lifted her hand back in the air and waved.

Sophie and Alex, then, were alone.

"I like your sister. She is ... perceptive."

"I wouldn't have said so," Sophie corrected peevishly.

His laugh was like warm caramel on her skin. She expelled a breath and forced herself to face him. "How was New York?"

"Exhausting," he responded honestly. "I would have called, except ..."

Sophie nodded quickly, but she didn't believe him. "Don't worry about it. I had Liv. We've been having a great time."

He had no doubt, and yet her attitude bothered him. "Have you missed me at all?"

She lifted a hand and toyed with her necklace. She wanted to deny it, because she wasn't sure he deserved her slavish devotion. But she found herself nodding. "Alex, I wanted to talk to you that day, but you'd left already."

He nodded, his eyes dark in his face. "I needed to get out of here."

"You were angry with me. And I'd like to know why."

God, but she had gall! To put him on the spot and ask to know what had bothered him, when surely she knew how very wrong her behaviour was! "I am quite certain you already know why," he drawled, reaching down and linking his fingers through hers. Warm heat travelled the length of her arm from where they were joined. She looked down at their clasped hands, as if she might see a source of heat, like flame or fire.

She had a feeling that she was sinking into volcanic lava. Did he know? Could she gamble that he didn't? And if it wasn't about Helena, then what?

"I don't know why," she said finally. For she only suspected, and the more she thought about it, the more his anger didn't seem to fit the situation. If he had discovered the truth about Helena, surely he would have peppered her with questions to ascertain the degree of Helena's depression.

"I see." He lifted her hand to his lips and pressed his teeth lightly into the soft pad of her thumb. "And so we will continue to pretend."

Sophie's heart turned over in her chest. "Alex, this is killing me. Please talk to me."

Alex had thought about doing just that. But wouldn't it simply give her the opportunity to go back to Eric? No. Alex needed to hold onto his wife until he was certain Helena's marriage was safe. "I do not wish to talk to you right now," he murmured, slipping a finger through the straps of her swimmers and gliding the top down her arms.

"Alex," she groaned, for her insides were already churning with pleasurable anticipation at his touch. "We have to talk."

He put an arm around her waist and guided her away from the pool, towards the villa. The side entrance led to the room he used for business, and beyond them, there was a narrow staircase. He led her up it until they reached yet another bedroom.

"When you are ready to talk honestly to me, I will listen."

She stared at him and felt a strange prickle of concern. "Why do I get the feeling you're playing me somehow?"

His smile was bleak. "Because I am."

Sophie tried to think of something to say, but he brought his mouth down to one of her nipples and rational thought became increasingly difficult.

"Alex," she lifted her hands, meaning to push him away, but they gripped the lapels of his shirt instead. "I don't understand."

"Does it matter now? In this moment, do you care?"

"I care," she shuddered as he transferred his mouth to her other breast.

"Do you want me to stop, so that we can speak?"

"No," she responded instantly, her breath coming in ragged spurts now. "There will be time ... later."

"Yes. The rest of our lives, remember?" His ironical tone wasn't lost on her. It was simply subsumed by what they were about to share.

In contrast to several nights earlier, when they made love now, Alex was gentle and kind, careful to hold her lovingly as he moved her to the brink of passionate collapse. It was as if he was atoning for the way he'd taken her, only Sophie, traitorous, treacherous, sex-mad Sophie, was part-desperate for the intensity and strength he'd introduced her too.

As she felt herself tipping into climax, she dug her nails into his shoulder. "Fuck me, Alex."

He lifted his head so that he could stare into her eyes. His look was loaded with silent enquiry.

"Fuck me, Alex," she repeated, nodding slowly.

He ran a hand down her cheek. "I hurt you last time."

"No." A single tear slid out of the corner of one of her eyes and he watched it with a kick of remorse. "Your manner hurt me. Your anger hurt me. You didn't hurt me. Physically, you were ... amazing. It was amazing." Her cheeks flamed. Discussing their sex life was not something she'd ever find easy.

He shook his head, his eyes banking down on the emotions she was invoking. "I was angry. I do not ever want to hurt you, Sophie." It was a plea. A broken, angry, confused plea, and Sophie understood then that whatever he knew, whatever he felt, it was eating him alive too.

"Then don't." She pushed up on her elbows and kissed him. "I love you, Alex. Whatever else you think, you have to know that I married you because I love you."

He kissed her back, but he felt even less convinced of anything than ever. She was either an excellent liar, or she did indeed feel something for him. But love? Was this woman who had slept with two of her married employers truly capable of feeling love?

He made love to her with the desperate, aching need that was consuming him. He took her until she screamed with pleasure, and then he held her tight. Silently, while he held her to his chest, he begged whatever Gods were out there to work out a way to make his Siren truly belong to him.

And to absolve him of guilt for manipulating her into a marriage that, if she understood his true motivation, she wouldn't have wanted a bar of.

* * *

"Seriously the best Scotch I've ever had." Olivia cradled the glass in her hand, her legs curled beneath her. The man she'd come to meet had, over the previous two days, impressed her. She hadn't wanted to be caught up in his web, but Alessandro Petrides was an impressive specimen. Funny, engaging, intelligent, gorgeous and generous, he had made her feel completely at ease, and had even insisted on his private jet taking her over to Vegas. "It is, forever, at your disposal. Any time you need it, simply call Sophie and she can arrange it."

Sophie had been oddly touched by the gesture, for it provided some of the reassurance that she was desperately seeking. Beside their bed, which was practically burning up from the heat of their connection, he spoke to her with the same civil politeness he was employing with Olivia. In fact, perhaps even less!

She watched the two of them with a sense of exclusion.

"You should try some Soph."

Sophie wrinkled her nose. "I'm still recovering from our champagne bonanza," she said with a shrug.

"Bonanza." Olivia shook her head with mock disappointment. "My sister just can't handle her liquor, I'm afraid."

"I have noticed," he said with a laugh. "Where will you stay in Vegas?"

"I don't know." She grinned. "That's part of the fun."

"We have a home there. Of course you may ..."

"No, no." Olivia held up a finger. She'd had several wines with dinner and three different scotches with Alex afterwards, and yet she seemed completely in control. "You're not going to deprive me of my fun."

He arched a brow inquisitively.

Sophie smiled, despite the gnawing certainty that something was very badly wrong in her marriage. "Liv loves the thrill of destitution. She's not a big believer in having money in the bank, nor a steady job."

"I see." He smiled, but it didn't quite reach his eyes. Sophie understood, too late, what she'd said wrong. It was not a joke to him. Alex had lived that life. He'd been destitute for real, and he knew, better than most, that it was not funny, nor was it fun. She searched for something to say – anything – to move the conversation forward before Olivia could add something else to the insensitive remark. "I've never been to Vegas."

"I thought you went with Edwin," Liv remarked, lifting a finger to her chin thoughtfully. "Didn't you go when he had that conference?"

Sophie's eyes flew to Olivia's with shock. She knew they couldn't speak of her former employer!

Alex, still in his chair, was instantly alert. He saw the panic in Sophie's face.

"Edwin?" He aimed his query towards Olivia, who was far more communicative than his secretive wife.

"Sophie's boss back in Sydney. A real pig of a man, but you thought the world of him for a while."

Sophie winced at the poor choice of words.

"I see," Alex nodded, but Sophie could see that he didn't.

"Liv," Sophie's voice held a warning, but Olivia ignored it. She might have seemed unaffected by the alcohol she'd imbibed, but of course she wasn't.

"Oh, come on. It's ancient history. Besides, you must have told Alex about him?" Before Sophie could reply, Liv turned back to Alex. "This guy was a real piece of work. He fell completely in love with Soph and got really creepy for a while there."

Alex, who had seen the report for himself, knew Olivia's version of events was incorrect, but he did a good job of pretending otherwise. "Creepy how?"

"Olivia." Sophie stood, and her face was completely white beneath her tan. "You must stop."

"Why?" She sat up straighter, as if realising for the first time that she'd said something wrong. "Oh, Sophie. What did I do? I'm sorry. I'm such a blabber mouth. I just presumed he knew."

"No," Sophie was bewildered.

"Because of the agreement. Right." She slapped her forehead. "No more scotch for me." She stood, her expression contrite. "Having dropped that messy little bombshell, I might absent myself now." She smiled weakly at Alex and then crossed to her sister. In a whisper, she said, "I'm so, so sorry."

"Don't worry about it." Sophie smiled kindly. "I know you didn't mean it."

She watched Olivia leave the room with a sinking heart. Confidentiality agreement or not, she certainly owed some explanation to her husband.

She toyed with her fingers and sighed. "It's not a big deal. And it was a long time ago. That's why I didn't tell you."

"Tell me now," he said quietly, fascinated to see how convincing she could be.

She nodded jerkily. "It was basically like Liv just said." She shook her head in frustration. "But he wasn't like it all along. In the last few months, he got a bit weird." Her cheeks flamed. "It's hard, when you're working as a nanny. Those lines can get blurred." She closed her eyes. "I've looked back and I've tried to see if I did something that encouraged him. I mean, I was always there, living with them, playing with the kids. It's really intimate. Maybe he thought I was encouraging him." She looked down at her tangled fingers. "I wasn't though. At least, not intentionally. When he ... made it obvious that he thought we were more than we actually were, I quit."

"How did he make this obvious?" Alex pushed. And though he knew his wife was creating a fiction to save her hide, he still felt a sharp pang of jealousy for this man.

She shook her head. "Details aren't important." Sophie didn't want to remember that night, when he'd come to her hotel room uninvited and drunk. It had taken all her strength and presence of mind to lock herself in the bathroom and wait until he'd calmed down.

"A secret, Sophie?"

"No." She bit down on her lip and her look was so intensely vulnerable that Alex wanted to pull her into his arms. "Just ... not something I like to talk about." She sighed. "The next day, I quit. He had me sign a confidentiality agreement."

"In exchange for what?" Alex pushed.

"Money." At his look of disappointment, she added quickly, "I used it for my airfare to London, and then gave the rest away. I didn't want a penny from him. I didn't want him thinking that he'd paid me off, and that what he did was therefore somehow okay."

"To whom?"

"To whom?" She repeated, lost by his question.

"To whom did you give the money?" He clarified impatiently.

"My sister Ava." Sophie decided that some secrets could be lifted. "She's a single mother. She runs our family vineyard and the little row of cottages we rent out for accommodation."

He arched a brow and Sophie didn't know what more he wanted her to say.

"I didn't tell you because I'm not really allowed to discuss it. And also because I hate to think about it." She fixed her gaze on his. "Even now, I wonder if I did something wrong. I'm ... a friendly person. Maybe I was too friendly."

Alex could have said dozens of things to assuage her worry, but he didn't. He wasn't sure he believed her version of events, given the dossier he'd received from his investigator. And yet, there were several sides to any story, and particularly this one. The wife had blabbed. Sophie had not. Sir Edwin Thomas had not. Perhaps the wife had put two and two together and got five.

In the same way he'd first thought Helena might have been mistaken, until he'd gone to London for himself to see the degree of affection between Eric and Sophie.

"Are you going to say anything?" She whispered, after several long minutes of silence had passed.

"Let's go to bed."

Sophie's heart sunk further. Yes. Her marriage was in a state of decline and she didn't know how to arrest it.

She put her hand in his, and with it, all her hopes. She loved him. Surely he would see that, and he would let go of whatever was bothering him.

CHAPTER EIGHT

"How long will you be away for?" Sophie was amazed by how well she kept the emotion from her voice. Liv had left them earlier that day, and now, Alex had lifted a few of his immaculate suits from the wardrobe and layered them into a hanger bag.

"I do not know yet."

"I see." She toyed with the ends of her hair and forced her gaze beyond him, to the window that framed the sea. "I was just thinking I might go back to London for a while."

He froze, his heart decelerating to a soft, slow thud, before cranking back to fever pitch. "What for." A statement, it showed that he was displeased. But she couldn't care. Her heart, her broken, aching heart, could not hurt her more than it already was.

"Why do you think?" She murmured.

He snapped his zipper to the top and spun around to face her. "No."

"No?" She mouthed the word with shock. "What do you mean, 'no'?"

He stared at her long and hard, and then walked slowly towards her. "I mean that I am not going to let you do it."

"Are you kidding me?" She stared at him as though he'd turned into a Martian. "I'm not your prisoner. You can't actually keep me here."

"No," he agreed. "But nor can I let you continue to ruin my sister's marriage."

The words hung between them like tiny little bullets. They sat heavy in the air and then flew swiftly towards Sophie. She staggered back as though she'd been hit, and reached for the edge of the bed. She sank into it weakly. "What are you talking about?"

Alex could have strangled himself, if it were at all physically possible. He had not intended to say so much to his wife, and yet it had simply blurted out. Now? What choice did he have but to have this discussion? Perhaps, if warned off, Sophie might choose not to go after Eric.

"I know about you and Eric."

She stared at him with a host of emotions storming across her face. "What do you know about me and Eric?" Her voice was barely a whisper.

He refused to feel sorry for her. The obvious discomfort was because of her actions and culpability, not his.

"I know that you and Eric, my friend, a man I trusted and cared for, have been having an affair. It is making Helena miserable. I will not allow it to continue."

Sophie wrapped her arms around her waist, as realisation after realisation continued to explode in her brain. There was no affair, but she was chasing after him, down a rabbit hole into the bizarre reality she now realised he'd been inhabiting. "How would you stop it?" She wondered aloud. "I mean, you did stop it, didn't you? By marrying me... That's what you think?" She closed her eyes. "Oh my God. Am I the most gullible idiot in the world or what?" She stood up but swayed a little on her legs and had to sit back down again.

His mouth was grim. "I needed to remove you from the situation."

She felt as though she was about to be sick, but she had no intention of letting him see how completely he'd devastated her.

"You married me because you believed Eric and I were having an affair and you wanted to end it. Right?"

His temper spiked. "I married you because I *knew* you and Eric to be engaged in an affair."

"How did you know?" She pushed, her body limp-feeling.

"That is hardly relevant."

Sophie nodded slowly. "I guess not." Tears sparkled in her eyes. She steeled herself to find a hidden reserve of strength, and tried to stand again. When she spoke, her words were little more than a whisper, but he heard them clearly. "Except that you were wrong. Completely wrong."

"Even now, you lie to me? When I know the truth?"

"You don't know the truth," she said thickly. "But I'm glad I finally do."

A sob was threatening in her chest. She swallowed it back, but it made her throat ache.

His voice was a soft plea – unusual for a man like Alex. "You will ruin her life if you continue this."

Sophie was numb to her core. "I'm not involved with Eric. He loves your sister."

"Bullshit. He loves you. I've seen the two of you together. I saw him come from your room late at night. I heard you speaking to him on the phone a few weeks ago. Talking about the secret you must keep from me, because Helena and I could never forgive the two of you. Do not make me think worse of you now, Sophie, by failing to own up to what you have done."

Her laugh was bitter. "You're sick, do you know that?" She moved to her wardrobe on autopilot and scanned it for her more practical clothes. She grabbed things at random. Jeans. A shirt. A dress. Shoes. And then, her arms full, she threw them onto the bed while she hunted around for a bag.

"I have already told you that I am protective of Helena. She was miserable about the affair. She begged me to help."

Sophie sniffed as she stuffed her clothes into the suitcase. Everything would need to be ironed again, and she hated ironing, but packing neatly would take time, and she couldn't stay in the house a moment longer.

"There was no affair," she said again, zipping the suitcase up ferociously. It snagged her nail and she swore.

"Then what secret are you and Eric huddling over so conscientiously. What were the 'late night sessions' you spoke of engaging in with him?"

Sophie thought about lying to Alex, to protect Eric further, but in that moment, she hated Eric and Helena almost as much as she did her husband.

With a voice that was surprisingly calm, and eyes that were devoid now of feeling, she faced her husband and said, "Your sister isn't well. I believe she has severe depression. Eric is beside himself with worry. We would meet secretly to discuss what we had noticed and plan a way to help her."

Alex was as still as a statue. Only a muscle that ticked in his cheek showed that he felt any emotion. "Another lie."

"No." She continued in the same tone. "I would never lie about something like this." She swallowed another sob. "Helena needs help. But Eric was worried that if he told you, you'd go all crazy and act like an overbearing bastard. Actually, he clearly had a point." She lifted the bag over her shoulder.

"Where are you going?" He demanded.

"Away."

"Where?"

She laughed, a harsh, jangling sound. "Nowhere you'll be able to find me. I need time to myself."

"Sophie, you need to tell me what you mean about Helena."

"No, I don't. I don't need to do any damn thing you say." She pulled the bag over her shoulder. She moved towards the door, a strange emptiness spreading through her. "Did you really marry me just for the sake of your sister?"

He stared at her long and hard; his silence, though, spoke volumes.

"Okay." She could no longer stop the tears that were moistening her eyes from falling. She turned around and walked back to him. She tilted her face up to his. "You need to know that I married you because I loved you completely. You need to know that, because one day, you're going to realise that I'm telling the truth. And on that day, you deserve to feel as guilty as hell for using me like this." She saw the shock on his face with some satisfaction. "I don't love you anymore. In fact, I don't think I ever really knew you." Her cheeks were wet and her chest was heaving with the pain of breathing. "Goodbye."

"You cannot leave like this. We have to discuss ..."

"I beg your pardon." She paused just outside the door. "We have nothing to discuss. Everything we were was a lie."

Downstairs, in the long hallway, she pulled her credit cards out of her wallet and left them on the mantle. Her ring she added to the pile of things she no longer needed. They belonged to Alex's wife, and Alex's wife had just been some poor sucker who'd allowed herself to be manipulated into believing in love.

That woman was not Sophie anymore.

She would never believe in love again.

CHAPTER NINE

"I am afraid I do not comprehend what you are saying." Alex sat down in his leather office chair with a gnawing sense of disbelief. Could this be some kind of trick? Had Sophie fooled her replacement into spreading these lies?

"I'm sorry, sir, but you asked me to report anything untoward to you."

Yes, he had, but he'd meant a secret love affair between Eric and Sophie. Not this, of all things.

Elaine continued, when Alex didn't speak. "I believe your sister needs to see a specialist. Perhaps even to be admitted to hospital for a time."

"And on what do you base this conclusion?"

"I have seen it before. The sense of disconnection is a hallmark. Your sister is ... vacant ... even when she is with the children."

"She's not maternal," he countered firmly.

"This is different, sir."

He stared out of the window. Sophie had warned him. And he'd ignored her. He hadn't wanted to believe that she might have been right.

Sophie. Had she really been gone three weeks already? He lifted her ring from his desk without noticing that he was doing it. It was a constant reflex with him these days. He would stare at it and remember the way her face had looked at it in complete confusion, the first time he'd shown it to her. The way she had insisted it was far more than she needed. The way she'd said she loved it, because he'd chosen it.

His gut twisted.

Everything in the house reminded Alex of Sophie. Everything. She was everywhere he looked, and yet she was nowhere.

"Are the children affected?"

"On some level, certainly. There is a wariness with them. An obvious preference for their father and me. They try to orchestrate outings that exclude their mother, as though they're attempting to form a family unit with me and Eric."

Alex had seen all this before. Only he'd blamed Sophie. He'd blamed Sophie and Eric. "And what do you do?"

"I do as they wish, of course. Their emotional wellbeing is my primary goal. I do, however, think you need to enable support for your sister."

"I see."

He lifted the ring to his cheek. Where was Sophie? He knew only that Harry had taken her to the airport, and that she hadn't touched his bank accounts since leaving.

He didn't know where she was living, and on what money she was surviving. Did she have savings? Did she have a job? Did she have a comfortable home? The thought of Sophie in discomfort or squalor flooded him with anger.

"Elaine, I'm going to come to London. Do not mention this to Eric until I arrive. I will ... require an element of surprise."

His mind made up, he set about organising the logistics. For a man like Alex, this was not difficult. With an army of staff and a jet at his disposal, it was only a matter of hours before he was back in London; staring at the house he'd first seen her. Sophie.

Then, he'd come to London to help his sister.

And now, he was there on the same chore, but with a far different goal in mind.

How long had this been going on? How long had Eric suspected? And why hadn't he taken Alex into his confidence? What had Sophie said? Eric had been afraid Alex would take over. Well, he was damned right about that. Alex had every intention of helping his sister, to hell with what Eric thought.

In the end, Eric was actually relieved that Alex had swept in and taken over. Helena, too, seemed finally glad that someone was telling her what to do in order to feel better. An exceptional facility accepted her immediately – another benefit of being Alessandros Petrides – and the day after she'd left, Alex found himself sitting on the sofa, a scotch in one hand, and an expression of despair on his face. It was the same sofa he'd first seen Sophie scrambling under and he wished he could reach back through time to that moment and slap himself for not seeing her as she really was.

"Eric, I need to know."

"To know what?" The other man was similarly bleak.

"About you and Sophie."

"What about me and Sophie?" He was distracted, staring at the floor.

Alex ran a hand over his stubbled chin. "Helena believed the two of you were having an affair."

That caught Eric's attention. "She ... what?"

If Alex needed any further confirmation of just how badly he'd got it wrong, his friend's expression offered it. He spoke matter-of-factly. "Helena called me. Two months ago. It is why I came to London. She asked me to intervene." The words tasted horrible in his mouth. Everything about it was disgusting to him.

"I can't believe it. Poor Helena."

"Poor Helena?" Alex shook his head. "Poor Sophie."

"Why? Why poor Sophie?" Eric swirled his glass; the ice clinked against its edges.

Alex had successfully kept news of his separation from reaching his sister and her husband. But now, as Eric regarded his old friend carefully, something like suspicion moved within him.

"Alessandro? What are you talking about?"

He swallowed, so that his Adam's apple moved visibly. "It does not matter. It's my problem to resolve." He fixed his friend with a serious stare. "Why didn't you tell me any of this?" If only Eric had confided in him! So much of this could have been avoided.

"No offence, mate, but you're the last person I would have told." He lifted a hand to silence Alex's imminent objection. "Helena wouldn't even acknowledge she had a problem. It was a bloody nightmare. I didn't want you to think I couldn't look after her." His eyes were haunted. "I worried you might think I couldn't make her happy."

Alex blanked out his feeling of pain.

"Sophie was wonderful," Eric sighed heavily. "You know what she's like. Such a gem. She became a part of our family instantly. She had only been here two days when she realised what was going on."

"How?" His voice was raspy; his heart was hammering heavily in his chest. "How did she know, when I, Helena's own brother, never realised anything was amiss?"

"Don't beat yourself up. I was slow on the uptake too."

"I do not understand how Sophie realised though. Helena held it together so well."

"Not when you spent a lot of time with her. The cracks were there."

"But Sophie didn't know her before."

"No. But her sister Ava had post-natal depression after her daughter was born. As you no doubt know, it was a very harrowing time for Sophie and she was able to spot the symptoms easily."

Alex shifted his weight and sipped his scotch because he couldn't meet his friend's eyes.

"I saw you coming out of her room that night."

"What night?" Eric queried diffidently.

"The night I proposed to her. It was late. She was hardly dressed."

"Oh. Wasn't she?" His gaze narrowed. "You can't seriously think I'd cheat on your sister? And with our nanny?"

"Sophie is more than just a nanny," Alex retorted angrily. "She's beautiful. She's ... I thought ... I presumed you would have found her irresistible."

"Like you did?" Eric queried with a disappointed smile.

Alex nodded warily.

"I'm telling you, mate, she's a stunner, but I've only ever had eyes for your sister."

"But you were in her room."

"Yeah." He nodded. "She borrowed money."

Alex stared at him, silently prompting Eric to continue.

"I told her I'd give it to her, but she insisted she wanted it to be a present for the kids, from her."

"What?"

"That's what she wanted the money for. To buy tickets to a show for the kids." He shook his head. "Your wife's all heart."

Alex nodded. His wife, all heart or not, was missing. And he could no longer keep it to himself, because he needed his friend's help.

* * *

Sophie had fine drops of paint splattered down the front of her shirt, and her blonde hair had copped a fair few spots of it too. She ran a hand over it and grimaced. It didn't matter. It was just paint.

London was, at any time of the year, her favourite place in the world. But now, in the lead up to Christmas, it was more beautiful than anything she'd ever seen. The streets of Mayfair were decked out in sparkly fairy lights overhead, and even now, in the early evening, it glistened with magic, snow and pale cream moonlight.

The bar was underground. Sophie paused at the top of the stairs while she slipped her gloves off and pushed them into her handbag, and then she began to move downward.

It was absolutely packed with the after-work crowd. Sophie weaved through the people determinedly, heading for the shining wooden bar.

She ordered a bottle of wine, though she didn't feel like drinking, and took up a table near the window. The associations gave her a bad case of nerves, but she couldn't wait to see Eric again, and to hear about the boys. She stared at the table top, and tried to relax. But the feeling of merriment that surrounded her was absolutely at odds with her deep well of grief.

Christmas would be here soon. And she would spend it alone. No Liv, for she seemed to have disappeared into technological thin air. Ditto Ava, who was probably trying to work out just how the hell to conceal Milly from Cristiano while he was physically on the same property as them.

And no Alex.

She pushed aside the well of pain.

It was only one year, and truly, it was just another day. What did it matter that she'd always loved the festive season? That it was a highlight of her year to decorate the tree and make mince pies and pudding?

None of that mattered.

A man jostled behind her and Sophie smiled up at him blandly then stared back at her empty glass. She might as well at least pour some wine, so that it was obvious she was waiting for someone.

She lifted the bottle at the exact moment Alex cleared into her view, and she would have dropped it to the floor had he not reached for it with lightning fast reflexes.

"Alex." Her voice was barely there. She cleared her throat and tried again. "What are you doing here?" She stared at him hungrily. He looked so good. Good enough to eat. But he was the devil. A bastard in disguise; a man who had hurt her wilfully and knowingly. She squared her shoulders and stared at him coldly. "I'm waiting for someone."

"Eric is not coming."

Sophie closed her eyes on the wave of despair. Suddenly, the friend she'd been longing to see had evaporated, and in his place was the enemy. "He told you."

"Yes."

Sophie was furious. Betrayed and angry. She scraped her chair back and stood, then grabbed her handbag from the floor. "Go to hell."

He stood up and blocked her from leaving. "I'm there, believe me."

"I don't believe you. I will never believe anything you say again."

"We need to talk."

"No." She glared at him defiantly. "I don't want to talk to you, or I would have called you. Don't you get that?"

"Sophie, I know that you were telling the truth."

She stared at him for a long time, and then finally, she laughed. It was a hollow cackle. "So? Is that supposed to make me forgive you? Because now you see that I would never in a million years hook up with a married guy?"

"I had you investigated. I got a … wrong, as it turns out … report about your work in Sydney."

"Oh my God." She sat down, simply because she felt shock assailing her body and taking her strength. Her legs were jelly. "You are some kind of sick bastard, aren't you? You knew about Edwin all along?"

"Yes." He crouched down before her. "I did. And I am. You must understand that I have spent my life being defensive and protective. These habits are not easily given away."

She clenched her teeth. "I don't want to hear it."

"Please, Sophie …"

"No." She glared at him. "Do you understand what you did?"

His heart twisted painfully inside his muscled chest. "Yes."

"No, you don't." She stood, and this time, anger propelled her forward. "You aren't the only one who has a past. I lost my mum. And I had to quit a job I loved because the guy basically attacked me. And I've been worried sick about Helena, and trying to help Eric, and loving those boys, and then I met you, and I'd never known anything like it. I was so blown away by how much I loved you, and how right it felt. I didn't doubt for even one second that you felt the same way."

"But I did, Sophie, I just didn't realise it."

"No." She laughed, and kept walking, back up the stairs and into the freezing cold night. "You wish that you had, because that would make you feel better. You hate that you were wrong about everything, because deep down, you think of yourself as morally superior to everyone on earth. But you aren't. You used me, and you treated me like dirt. I didn't deserve that." Tears sparkled on her long lashes. "And you're here now because you want me to make it better for you. I'm not going to." His expression was scored with emotion. But she ignored his hurt. "It's over."

He swallowed. "Please, let me talk with you. Just have dinner with me, at least, and hear what I say. I have words in my mind that I cannot contain. I must talk to you."

She sobbed, as the dam of emotion threatened to burst completely. "I don't want to hear them. Nothing you say matters. Don't you get it? I know that there are no words that will fix this."

"Sophie," he groaned, and reached for her hand, but she flinched away violently.

"I only came to see Eric. I shouldn't have called him. I had no idea he would tell you, or I would have found another way to get in touch. I just wanted to hear about the boys." Her voice cracked and she whipped her face away, angry at herself for showing such intense vulnerability to this man.

"Helena is in hospital. I am spending time in London while she recovers."

Sophie stared at him, and relief that the truth was finally out in the open was a welcome wave.

"You knew about her depression. You understood where I was blind."

What could she say to that? Nothing. She was silent.

"Our childhood has left marks on her. She is anxious. She has underlying issues that need to be addressed. She will get that time now to unravel the burdens our years of living rough left on her. She will get help, finally."

Sophie nodded; she had no words to describe how glad she was. "How are Ian and John?"

"They are missing their mother; and they are missing you. Their new nanny is good to them, but she does not read Peter Pan."

Sophie didn't smile. She'd lost the ability. "I have a new family now."

"You work for someone else?" It displeased him and frustrated him all at once.

"Temporarily. Yes."

"Yet you are here."

"Yes."

And for the first time he saw the paint in her hair and on her shirt and he smiled. "I am asking you only for dinner."

His smile hardened her heart. It had been his smile that had turned her admiration into love. Her longing from lust to love. "And I am asking you to leave me alone."

"I can't do that."

"Don't you get it, Alex? You broke what I felt for you beyond repair. You made it ridiculous and untenable. It's not just that I needed time to get over it. To forgive you. There is no forgiving this."

"Only because you think I tricked you into marriage," he murmured sharply, aware that the street was busy.

"You *told* me that's what you did!"

"And maybe I even believed it then. But Sophie, how could I not love you?"

"Don't!" She stamped her foot. "Don't use that word. You have no idea what it is to love someone."

"I am telling you the truth …"

She lifted a hand and slapped his cheek hard, and then she sobbed. Grief and shock mingled inside of her. "Don't. Just ... don't." She spun on her heel and ran down the street. It was crowded but she was slight and she weaved effortlessly through the hoards of commuters. Only at the corner, with traffic flying in all directions, was she forced to pause.

Alex, one hand lifted to his burning cheek, strode purposefully down the pavement towards her. He didn't know what to do to fix this, but he had to get through to her. He watched as his wife looked in both directions, and then flicked her head over her shoulder, to see where he was. Her eyes clutched to his, and then her mouth opened and she winced.

It all happened incredibly fast. One moment she was looking at him in surprise, and the next she was crumpling to the footpath. He reached her just in time to thrust a hand beneath her head and save it from hitting the ground. But there was still blood beneath her. Where was it coming from? Had something hit her? A car? A bike?

With fingers that shook, he pulled his phone from his pocket and dialled triple nine. The ambulance appeared swiftly, but Sophie did not properly regain consciousness.

The next two hours passed in a blur. Despite the fact they were married, Alex was kept in the waiting room. The floor was linoleum, the walls were pale blue and a fluorescent light flickered with troublesome inconsistency.

No one ever kept Alex waiting. For many years, doors had opened swiftly as he approached them. People paused conversations to hear what he had to say.

And yet hospitals and illnesses were levellers like no other.

With Sophie in a room, having suffered God knew what kind of accident, he was simply a man, waiting to hear about the woman he loved.

And the waiting was agonising.

Finally, when Alex was about to jump out of his skin, a doctor appeared and called his name.

"Hello, I'm Maggie." Her expression was perennially kind. She had a soft easiness to her that spoke of many such conversations.

Alex nodded, his face ashen. Internally, he braced for bad news.

"Your wife will be fine."

He expelled the breath he'd been holding; and he could have hugged the calm, gentle doctor. "Can I see her?"

Maggie shook her head. "I'm sorry, not yet." Maggie held a hand out and indicated that he should follow her.

"What happened to her? What is it?"

"There's no easy way to tell you this." Her expression softened even further. If she employed any more sympathy, she would turn into a giant Hallmark card. Fear pulsed through him. It was bad news. The doctor was weighing up her words, summing him up for how much he could take.

"Tell me," he commanded. He needed to know.

Maggie nodded. "I'm very sorry, Mr Petrides, but your wife lost the baby."

Alex stopped in his tracks and stared at her. "What are you saying? She was pregnant?"

Maggie consulted her charts. "Indeed. Around eight or nine weeks along, I'd say."

Alex closed his eyes on the wave of pain. For Sophie, and for him, and for the life they'd created, and lost. "Did she know?"

"I … I'm not sure," Maggie said quizzically. "You didn't?"

"No." He squared his shoulders. "I must see her, please."

"She's still groggy from the anaesthetic."

"I *need* to see her," he responded, his chest hurting, his arms aching.

Maggie looked at him for a moment and then nodded. "She mustn't be tired out, though. She's undergone a significant trauma and procedure, and her body is weak."

"Doctor, why did she lose the baby?" He asked, just outside the door to Sophie's room.

Maggie's look was carefully blanked of emotion. She spoke slowly, to drum the meaning of her words into him. "There is no hard and fast explanation. Sometimes, it just happens. The important thing to remember is that it doesn't mean you will not be able to conceive and carry a pregnancy to term."

Alex's gut clenched. He knew he wasn't likely to get a second chance with Sophie. Even before this happened, she had been far too devastated by his actions to forgive him. And now? Everything was broken.

He pushed into Sophie's room and then stopped in his tracks at the sight of her. So pale and weak, against the hospital issue pillows.

Her eyes were bleak when they landed on him, but she didn't look away.

"I didn't know." She answered his unspoken question, and a sob tore from her. "I had no idea."

Alex nodded. "That does not matter." He moved to her, but when he put a hand on her head, she made a sound of disgust.

"Don't touch me. I can't bear it. I can't bear to look at you." She turned away from him, and stared out of the window.

"I need to be with you."

"Well, I need you not to be."

"What do you need? What else? If not me, what?"

"I don't know." She sobbed. "My phone. I need to talk to my sisters."

"Of course. Would they fly to you? I can send a jet ..."

"No." She closed her eyes. "I don't want to scare them. I'll be fine. I just want to ... speak with them. About anything. They always make me feel better."

Alex knew then that he wanted to be that person to Sophie. The one person who could take away any evil, or at least endure it by her side.

"What about the family you work with? Can I call them for you?"

"Oh, goodness. Yes." She shook her head. "I mean, *no*. But I'll need to notify them. Please just get my phone."

He nodded, and pulled it from her bag. Even the sight of it, with its bright pink case, made his stomach twist with memory. He listened as she spoke, so eloquently and calmly, and yet perfectly vaguely, explaining that she couldn't work for a time.

She disconnected the call but kept the phone clasped in her lap.

"Are you going to call your sisters?" He prompted, reclining with assumed indolence against the wall.

Sophie stared at the phone and shook her head. She wanted to hear their voices more than anything in the world, but she knew that one word from Ava and she'd burst into tears. It would be the same with Liv. They would know something bad had happened, and they would worry themselves sick.

She lifted bleak eyes to his face. "You can go, Alex. I'd rather be alone."

"Are you going to slap me again?" He said mockingly, lifting his hand to his cheek.

She might have smiled, in a past life. She didn't now.

Her lips quivered as she flipped her head on the pillow and eyed him warily. "I don't want you to see me like this."

A muscle flexed in his jaw. He didn't say anything, and after a moment, Sophie gave up fighting. She closed her eyes and gave into the tears.

A baby. Their baby. How had she not known? Why hadn't she realised?

And why had she lost it?

When Alex put a hand on her head and stroked it softly, she didn't move away. She allowed herself to take comfort from the contact, and to relish the touch.

Though she would have sworn she wasn't tired, Sophie was asleep within minutes. The next thing she knew, it was somewhere in the middle of the night. The room was mostly darkened, but for the faint electric glow cast by the hospital's instruments. The sleeping shape of Alex was visible hunched in one of the upright chairs. She looked at him and hardened her heart.

He was there because he felt guilty. A burden of responsibility, like he felt with Helena. That wasn't the same thing as love. Wanting to fix someone and take over their life didn't equate to caring.

She tried to rearrange herself, to find a more comfortable position, but she was too uncomfortable, and so she flopped back as she'd been.

When the morning light broke through the window, Alex was awake, and looking far more like his normal self. Despite the fact he still wore the previous day's clothes, he was fresh and vibrant and heart-stoppingly, unfairly beautiful.

"Good morning," he spoke quietly, as though he feared she might yell at him. Except Alex wasn't afraid of anything, least of all her.

Sophie smiled at him out of habit, and then immediately regretted it.

"How do you feel?"

Empty. Alone. Cold. "I'm fine."

He held a plastic beaker of water out to her; Sophie took it and drank gratefully.

"The doctor will be in soon. Would you like breakfast? Coffee?"

Sophie shook her head.

"Tea?"

Her eyes lifted to his and she nodded. "Thanks."

He left the room and her sense of aloneness intensified. When first she'd moved to London, she had thought it the most beautiful place on earth. She had immediately known she wouldn't ever think of Casa Celli as home again. But now, after the last few months, Sophie craved the peace and solitude of the vineyards to lick her wounds and recover.

She needed the company of her sisters and the familiarity of her youth.

At least, a part of her did.

Alex was back within moments, carrying a fine bone porcelain cup of tea. From where he'd procured it, she couldn't have guessed. Presumably one of the nurses had decided the standard chipped mugs in the kitchen weren't good enough for a man such as him.

"Thank you," she murmured as he passed it over. Sophie held it in both hands, taking comfort from the warmth.

She sipped and he watched, his expression indecipherable.

Another doctor arrived shortly after she had finished drinking. He was tall and skinny, wiry like a rake, with fine hair that wisped over his brow. His eyes were intelligent and his face lined. Sophie warmed to him immediately.

"Good morning, Mrs Petrides. How are you today?"

"Fine, thanks." It was an answer given by rote. The doctor disregarded it.

"Any pain? Discomfort?"

"Yes. Yes." Her eyes lifted to Alex and he understood. She didn't want him there. She was closing him out. But he needed to be with her. Didn't she understand that? Didn't she care?

"That's to be expected." He pulled back the bed sheet to reveal Sophie's hospital gown clad body. "May I?"

She nodded, and the doctor began to move his hands over Sophie's abdomen. She lay there, staring at the ceiling, ignoring Alex and wishing she was anywhere else.

"Excellent." He returned the sheet and smiled, first at Sophie and then at Alex. "You'll be discharged this morning. I'm writing you a script for pain relief. Don't be a hero. It's perfectly fine to take when recovering from something like this." He handed the script to her and she held it folded in her fingertips. "You'll need to take a few days to recover. I mean complete recovery. Lying on the sofa, watching those terrible Real Housewife programs my wife is obsessed with."

She smiled despite her sense of oddness and grief.

"Mr Petrides, there's paperwork at the front you can complete when you're ready. If you need any nursing assistance, mention it to the clerk."

"None will be necessary," he said, his eyes not leaving Sophie's face.

"Excellent. Good luck to you, Mrs Petrides." He nodded at Alex and then disappeared.

Because Sophie knew Alex, she knew what he was planning, and she decided to be proactive from the get go. "You can help me get a cab. That would be great."

"You will be coming home with me."

"No, I won't." She folded her arms across her chest. "I'm not going to stay with you."

His mouth was a grim line as he settled on the edge of the bed. "Aren't you?" He reached forward and tucked her hair behind her ear.

"I can't." She unfolded her arms and fidgeted with her fingers. "Please just go, Alex. You don't need to be here."

"This is exactly where I need to be."

She closed her eyes. "I can't go back to your house. I can't ever step foot in it again. Surely you can see that it would be more harmful to me than anything else."

"Fine," he didn't see any sense in arguing the point. "I'll hire a hotel room. But I am going to take care of you. I feel responsible, Sophie. Please don't deny me the opportunity to help you now."

She thought about telling him that he could help by leaving her alone for good. That he could help by never going near her again. But a part of her, even then, was afraid he might do it if she asked often enough.

"Why?" She said instead. "Why can't you just go?"

He lifted her hand and rubbed her empty ring finger. There was a very feint indent from where she'd worn the jewellery for a brief time.

"Because you are my wife."

Her eyes swept shut at his words and her heart iced over. "A stupid joke," she muttered angrily.

"No. A clever twist of fate."

She shook her head.

"Do you know why I thought the worst of you Sophie? Why I believed you to have engaged in affairs with both Eric and the man from Sydney?"

"Because you're suspicious, cynical and untrusting?"

His lip twisted in a half-smile. "No. Because I fell in love with you the first moment I saw you, half hidden beneath the sofa. I loved you. Your voice, your energy, you. And how could any man not feel as I did? How could any man not see you and want you, as I did, with a total, full-body response?"

She blinked her eyes opened and stared at him as though he must surely have thought her to be some kind of idiot. "You're being ridiculous. You never loved me. I'd go so far as to say you hated me. Or you would never have gone through with this ridiculous plan to get me out of Helena's life."

"I loved you then, Sophie, and I love now. Do not argue with me. I always win. Eventually, you will accept that."

"Eventually ... Alex, it's over between us. I can't ... I won't ... forgive you."

"You will." His smile now was confident. "Stay here. I'll arrange for you to be checked out."

"Discharged," she muttered to his retreating back. "It's a hospital, not a hotel." She looked down at herself hopelessly, feeling more alone than she ever had in her whole life. "I have nothing to wear."

He frowned. Her clothes from yesterday were nowhere in sight. "Okay. Wait here."

"Do I have any other choice?" She queried with a sarcastic smile. And even then, angry with him and desperately miserable, she knew she was being rude and unfair. He had lost their baby too. And he was trying to help. Only she'd run out of any kind of generosity of spirit.

In barely no time at all, Alex was back clutching a dark green shopping bag. "Would you like help changing?"

She scowled at him, but didn't perceive any innuendo in the question.

He lifted his hands. "It was a genuine question, *agape mou.*"

"I'm fine." She took the bag without thanking him and peered inside. A black sweater and a pair of jeans were inside, complete with fresh underwear.

"Wait outside. Please."

"It was a serious offer of help, Sophie. You might be weak …"

"Then I'll buzz for a nurse," she said through gritted teeth.

"Okay. Fine." Alex tamped down on his frustration. He had lost any right to expect Sophie to simply be an unquestioning part of his life.

Out of nowhere, he thought back to the first week on Corfu, when she had been so happy she'd practically beamed with light and pleasure. He thought back to those heady days, when they'd shared one another's bodies and they'd talked and laughed as though they were careless and divinely euphoric. That brief, glimmering window of perfection that he'd smashed with his idiotic plan. What he wouldn't give to go back to that perfect oasis of time and hold it tight to his chest.

She dressed slowly, and Alex was on the verge of bursting back into her room when Sophie finally emerged. She'd washed her face and finger combed her hair, but she still looked a long way from well.

"Ready?" He smothered the worry from his voice, instinctively understanding that she didn't want sympathy. "My car is out the front."

She fell into step beside him, and the whole way, she knew she should separate herself from this man. Except she was tired, and she didn't feel great. It was only with enormous effort that she was able to walk without showing any physical signs of discomfort.

Alessandro Petrides was parked on double yellow lines just outside the hospital. His windshield had a host of paper on the front and he ripped them out impatiently.

"Alex," Sophie said sharply. "You're illegally parked."

The look he sent her was rich with disbelief. "Did you think I would waste time searching for a better spot while you were in hospital?"

She didn't let her heart swell. He felt guilty, that was all.

"You must have a thousand pounds in fines there."

"Worth it," he held her door open and waited patiently while she settled herself into the seat. He had to ball his hands into his pockets to stop from aiding her.

As soon as he took up his seat, the car felt smaller somehow.

"Ready?"

"You don't need to do this, Alex," she offered, in a final attempt to convince him she would be fine on her own.

His only response was to snap the car into gear and slip it out into traffic.

He'd booked the penthouse suite at an upmarket Knightsbridge hotel. It had views of Harrods in one direction and Hyde Park in the other. Once Sophie was settled onto the luxurious sofa, she thought she'd relax.

Only Alex was worse than a tightly coiled spring.

"Are you hungry yet?"

"No, thanks."

"How about tea? Would you like more tea?"

Sophie glared at him. "No."

"A movie then. What would you like to watch?"

"Nothing."

He came to sit at her feet. "A book perhaps? A magazine?"

Sophie couldn't help it. She burst out laughing. "Please, just stop! I just need to sit quietly for a while."

Alex nodded. "Okay. We can do that."

Sophie lay her head back on the fluffy pillows and stared at the ceiling. To his credit, Alex managed to stay silent, though he was anxious and eager to do something – anything – that would ease her suffering. Only every time he opened his mouth, he looked at her face and saw the ghosting emotions there. And it silenced him.

"How did I not realise I was pregnant?" She said finally, a disjointed sounding plea into the cavernous lounge area.

Alex lifted her feet onto his lap. He spoke slowly, with softness. "I've been doing some reading. Some women don't experience any symptoms."

"I felt just the same as normal. I mean, I guess I've been distracted because of ... everything ... but I haven't been sick, or tired, or sore anywhere."

He rubbed the soles of her feet, and watched as her features relaxed visible. "It seems that happens sometimes.

"But maybe if I'd known I could have done something. I could have been more careful."

Alex moved his hands to her legs and ran them over the jeans. "*Agape mou,* do not blame yourself." He dipped his head forward. "If anyone is responsible, then it is me. I upset you. I put you through a traumatic argument. I should have made you safe and happy for the rest of your life, instead of causing you to feel this way."

She cast him a doleful look. "I don't think that's possible of anyone, for anyone. In fact, it's frankly absurd to think you could do such a thing. Other people's happiness does not rest on your shoulders." And because she was tired and fraught, she spoke more frankly than she might otherwise have. "Not mine. Not Helena's."

He closed his eyes and nodded. He understood what she was referring to. "I have spent almost my whole life doing it though; fighting her fights and helping her when she asked. I didn't stop to question her request. And I should have. For both of your sakes."

Sophie settled further back into the pillows. "That you love your sister so much is to your credit. It's not your motivation I fault, so much as your method."

"I fault both. My motivation was to help her, but I didn't bother seeing what she really needed."

"Not your job," Sophie said simply. She was tired. The painkillers she'd had right before leaving the hospital must have been kicking in. Her eyes fluttered shut.

But Sophie was wrong. He crouched down beside her and stroked her forehead. He wasn't even sure if she was awake still, but he whispered to her, "I have loved you, with all that I am, from the first."

Her lips parted as though she was about to say something, but she didn't. She simply sighed and rolled over, turning away from him.

She slept on and off for most of the day, and Alex fretfully watched over her. But by evening, her cheeks had some colour in them and she was able to move more freely.

Alex took great care not to crowd her. He put the television on in the background and ordered a simple dinner that she could pick at when hungry, and then retired to his room on the pretence of work. Of course, he checked on her often, but he didn't want to rock the boat. For the moment, she had given up on asking him to leave her alone, and he hoped the truce would last.

The following morning, Sophie was even more like herself, though the reserve had returned. She was barely speaking to him, and was certainly unable to meet his eye.

It was out of desperation that he sought the most desperate measure of all.

9 November, 16.08pm
From: A Petrides
To: Ava, Olivia

I'm in need of the best Christmas pudding recipe ever. Sophie informs me it's yours. Please send it to me as a matter of urgency.

Yours,

A.P

Ava, who kept all of their sacred family recipes stored in a binder in the kitchen, was able to find it easily and send a copy back to Alex. And far away, on the other side of the world, she imagined her sister happy. She imagined her sister planning an English Christmas with the man she loved, and Ava took comfort from it in the midst of her own anxieties.

Sophie, meanwhile, was none the wiser that her sort-of husband had been emailing with her sisters. She was simply glad that Alex had stayed out for most of the afternoon. It had given her a chance to think, or at least to breathe. The problem was that when he was around, she was totally, utterly baffled. She knew that what he'd done was wrong, but it was almost impossible to hold onto her temper and resentment when he was staring at her with those enormous black eyes.

"Hello, *agape mou*," he said from the doorway, and Sophie looked towards him. Her heart began to hammer and she realised that she'd missed him. That, far from being glad he'd stayed out, she'd been counting the minutes until he returned. It infuriated her. He didn't deserve that. He deserved nothing from her!

"Hello." A small sounding word, from the depths of her doubts.

"How do you feel?"

Physically, she felt surprisingly well. She had the occasional cramp, and she was tired, but the bulk of how she was feeling was emotional. There, in her heart-space, she was a wreck. A ball of angst-ridden indecision and uncertainty.

"Sophie? You are okay?"

"Oh." She nodded clumsily. "Yes. I should be out of your hair soon, in fact."

At his thunderous look of disapproval, she stood. "Truly, Alex, I'm feeling much better. There's no reason for me to be here ..."

He placed the bags on the bench and moved steadily towards her. "There are many reasons for you to be here, and the most obvious one is that you are my wife."

She looked down at the thickly carpeted floor. "Nothing's changed since that day in Corfu."

"No, it hasn't." His eyes glittered darkly in his handsome face. "I love you as much now as I did then. I want you as my wife more now than that day, because I know now how empty I feel without you."

"You married me to break Eric and me up," she said sharply.

He laughed. "I think I really believed that too. But actually, dear Sophie, I married you because I couldn't live without you." He wrapped his arms around her waist. "I hated the idea of you and Eric together; not because I felt concern for my sister, but because I felt more jealousy and despair than I have ever known."

She shook her head slowly, and Alex took advantage of her silence.

"Now, I have a favour to ask of you."

"A favour?" She repeated in surprise, her frustration increasing.

"Yes. Do you feel able to sit here, at one of these stools?"

She looked at the kitchen suspiciously. "Why?"

"Well, I thought I would try my hand at your famous pudding. If you tell me what to do, that is."

Sophie felt a sting of emotion in her chest. He felt guilty. He was over-compensating. "You don't have to do this."

His smile was dazzling. "I want you to be my wife for the rest of my life. Do you get that?" He held her hands to his chest, and stared into her soul, hoping she would understand his sincerity. "I want to feel about Christmas as you do, and one day, I want our children to speak of you as you do your mother."

Tears clogged her eyes at his words, but Alex ploughed on.

"There will be children for us, Sophie. Not now, but one day. And they will be fierce and loyal and clever and beautiful, just as you are."

"I don't know if I can do this," she whispered darkly. "I loved you so much. I ignored all of the cautious words in my brain, because I just trusted so implicitly that my instincts were right. And I got burned." She swallowed back any further expansion on that subject. It was not necessary for her to detail how achingly sad she'd been.

"Yes." He nodded slowly. "And if I could take it all back, I would."

Her eyes were pools of doubt. "You're asking me to take a really big risk."

"Yes." He smiled at her encouragingly. "But slowly." He kissed the tip of her nose. "Just don't run away from me again. Let me show you how much you mean to me."

She exhaled slowly. "You're the one who ran away. You were gone most of our very short marriage."

"True."

"I don't want that. I don't want to miss you like I did." Her cheeks flamed at the honest admission, and she loathed it for its neediness."

"I wonder if you realised how I pined for you while I was gone."

Her voice was cold. "I find it hard to believe."

"Do you? Then you do not understand how much I cherish you. I ached for your touch and I craved your words. I went because I couldn't trust myself not to confess everything to you. I hoped, in my wildest imaginings, that you would absolve me of guilt and tell me Eric meant nothing to you. That he was in your past and I your future."

"Eric was nothing to me, even in my past. Just a friend I cared for. Whose wife I worried about. Nothing romantic. Nothing."

"I know that now."

"So why didn't you do that? Tell me the truth, and let me explain. It would have been resolved so easily if we'd talked. Instead you avoided me and raged at me and blamed me for everything."

"Because in my worst nightmares, which consumed me for the most part, I thought you would leave me instantly. That you would return to London and Eric, and Helena and I would have both lost the people we loved."

"That's ... the fears of a mad man."

"Yes. Absolutely. I was crazy. I completely agree."

She laughed despite herself. It felt good to laugh. "You believe me, don't you?"

"About everything." He shrugged. "I know it is taking the easy way out, but I think I knew all along that you weren't capable of doing what I accused you of."

"I would never break up a marriage." She couldn't help it. She lifted a hand and traced the outline of his lips. His stubble was like sandpaper. "I told you about my mum. She was the other woman in a marriage, and she was burned by it. She had no clue our father was married. But it doesn't change anything. She made us understand what a monumental mistake she had made. It's not in my biology to do what you thought I had."

"I know." He kissed her fingertips and his eyes begged her to believe him. "So will you include me in your secret pudding recipe now?"

She pursed her lips and pretended to think. "Well, that depends."

"Oh?" His expression was mocking, but his heart was barely moving. He was on tenterhooks, waiting to know if she would give him the second chance he so desperately needed.

"Our pudding is no laughing matter. It takes serious skills. I have to see if you've got what it takes before I make up my mind."

He exhaled with giddy relief. "Well then, Mrs Petrides, take a seat and give me a shot."

CHAPTER TEN

Christmas 2014, London.

"John!" Sophie burst out laughing. "You're going to spill everything."

John grinned at her. "Nope. I'm not. I promise."

She arched a brow and regarded Helena over the very confident little boy's head. Helena's eyes sparkled as she shrugged back.

As John reached the table, the tray he was haphazardly holding began to tilt, and would have tipped entirely were it not for Alex's quick reflexes. Alex gripped both sides and smiled gratefully at the little boy, who skipped off, apparently none the wiser.

"He's very ... helpful," Helena said apologetically.

"Oh, yes," Eric laughed, putting an arm around his wife's waist. "He's our little Jeeves."

Sophie leaned back in the leather chair. She didn't know it, but she was practically glowing with contentment. She missed her sisters like wildfire, but at the same time, she truly felt like she was home.

Alex lifted a flute of champagne from the table and handed it to Sophie. She held it and smiled up at him. She hadn't tasted champagne since the night in Corfu with Olivia, and the smell of the sweet bubbles brought pleasant memories back to her.

"So, let's run through our checklist." He crouched down beside her, his eyes teasing. "We decorated the tree a week ago. Does it meet your requirements?"

She looked beyond him at the beautiful alpine specimen and nodded. For someone who'd missed out on the special Christmas traditions, he'd caught up incredibly quickly. There were unique, custom-made decorations from Murano, and stars with their names on them, including her sisters and their parents. And he'd even had Ava send over a few of the very special heirloom decorations from the vineyard.

"And we've made an exceptional pudding."

"Well, we won't know that until we try it tonight," she argued.

"We've made gingerbread houses with the boys."

"And I ate a lot of dough."

"Yes," he shifted his eyes heavenward. "So much so that I thought you might be sick."

"Always a risk I'm willing to take."

"And I have a present for you."

She pouted. "But it's Christmas Eve. Presents come tomorrow."

"Perhaps. But I want you to have this. It's overdue."

That got her attention. "What is it?" She prompted curiously.

"It is in Eric's office."

"Oh."

Alex held his hands out for Sophie and she put hers in them.

"Can I come? Can I come?" John bounded behind them, and Ian followed him silently.

Alex shook his head. "Not this time, little one."

"I'm not little," he retorted fiercely, and Alex laughed.

"No, of course not. You're growing inches by the day." He shepherded Sophie into the study and closed the door on the two anxious little faces beyond.

"That was a tad cruel."

"Was it?"

"You know it was."

He grinned. "I am a selfish man. I wanted my wife to myself for this."

"What is it?" Her blood had begun to pound in her veins, as it always did when Alex and she were alone together. She wondered, distractedly, if that would ever change. If one day, she might even begin to take his gloriousness for granted.

He reached into his pocket and pulled out a small jewellery box. She recognised it. "My ring?"

He shook his head. "Try again."

Sophie took the box curiously and flipped the lid. Inside was the most perfect ring she'd ever seen. Dainty and elegant, a single circlet of yellow and white diamonds formed one band. It was sunny and it was pretty without being outrageously ostentatious.

"It suits you far better."

She nodded, tears in her eyes. "I'll say." He slipped it onto her finger and admired the effect.

"I beg you, Sophie, to be my wife. For the rest of our lives. Please know that I love you and will do anything you ever ask of me. Except leave you," he tacked on with a self-mocking smile. "Do not ask it of me, for I can't do it."

She laughed shakily. "Not much chance of that." She stared at the ring, her smile beaming. "Oh, Alex. It's so perfect. I truly love it." Her enormous blue eyes lifted to his face. "But ... what about my old ring? It's too gorgeous not to wear."

"Ah. I thought of that." He reached onto Eric's desk and lifted another velvet box. It was the same colour, but a slightly different size. Alex flipped the top and extended it to Sophie.

The solitaire was there, but it had been reset, and a chain attached, so that it formed a stunning pendant. "For special occasions," he said thickly.

"Perfect," she whispered once more.

"It is you who is perfect, Mrs Petrides. I just have to find a way to deserve you."

"Well," she pretended to consider that. "You do have a lifetime."

"And I intend to enjoy it."

He kissed her then with all the tenderness and love that he felt for her. Life was so much better than he'd ever hoped it could be, and it was all because he had this beautiful woman to share it with.

EPILOGUE

"I can't eat another thing!" Sophie groaned, pushing aside the bowl of pudding.

"But you haven't finished your third serve of pudding," Helena remarked with mock surprise.

"Don't laugh. I'm known for my ability to eat almost an entire one on my own. I live for pudding."

"If you love it so much, why not make it all year 'round, Soph?" Eric asked with a confused expression.

Sophie lifted her hands and clutched them to her chest in a gesture of mock pain. "You can't be serious. There's something very wrong with that idea. Pudding is wonderful, but it's just for Christmas time."

"And so you eat a whole year's worth in one sitting, just to avoid being preposterous?" Helena chimed in, her smile natural and beautiful on her elegant face.

"Yep. That's pretty much it."

Alex appeared in the door frame, a strange look on his face. "*Agape mou*, your sister is on the phone."

"She is? Which sister? Which phone?"

"Ava. In the kitchen."

Sophie smiled apologetically at Helena and Eric and moved swiftly through the townhouse.

"Hey! Merry Christmas!" She called down the phone line, and then froze when silence greeted her.

"Ava? What is it? Is it Milly? Cristiano?" There was silence as Ava mentally tallied all of the information she had kept from her sisters. Not intentionally. But she'd been so wrapped up in her own mess of a life that she hadn't known what to say. Only Olivia's email had forced her to make contact.

"No, no. It's Liv."

"Liv?"

Sophie felt a prickle of tension in her spine. She eased herself down at the table and took a deep breath. "What about Liv?"

"Didn't you see the email?"

"No. I haven't checked my phone all day. I'm sorry. What is it? What did she say?" Relief was an overpowering emotion when she realised that at least Olivia was alive, to be sending emails.

"You and she are as bad as each other," Ava grumbled angrily. "First you and Alessandro, and now Olivia."

"What about Olivia?"

"She says she's getting married to some guy. God, read the email."

Sophie shook her head. "I don't know how to while I'm talking to you. What did it say?"

Ava began to read, her voice shaking from shock. "I know I've been terrible with emails lately. I'm sorry, but when you read this, you're going to understand. I've met someone. Someone special. Oh boy, I hope you're both sitting down. Because I've just agreed to marry him. And that's not even the shocking part... "

Sophie dipped her head forward. "That's all she said?"

"Yes."

"But who? She never said anything? What? When? I just ... I don't understand."

"No. That makes two of us."

"Alex will be able to help."

"He can try, but Olivia's disappeared into thin air. The agency she worked for have no clue. Her home phone's not ringing. Her mobile's making a weird blee-blee-bloop noise whenever I call it."

"No, she wouldn't do that to us. She'll be in touch. Soon, too. This is Liv! She's the glue! Come on, Ava. She'll be okay."

"She's too bloody trusting is what she is. Any guy with a smile and a nice car and she's sold."

"She's not that bad."

"Yes she is. I'm not saying it to be prickly, but because it's the truth."

Sophie pressed her lips together. "I'll see what Alex can find out."

"Keep me posted."

"Sure."

"Ava?"

"Yeah?"

"Did Milly get the presents I sent?"

There was silence for a slight moment too long. It struck Sophie as odd. But then again, Ava was in a strange mood. Her worry about Olivia was obvious.

"Yeah, she loved them. She's resting now or I'd put her on to say thanks."

"I'll catch her tomorrow."

"Sure."

"Try not to worry, Aves. Liv's got a good head on her shoulders. She'll be okay."

Ava disconnected the call without responding, and Sophie silently echoed her sister's desperation. For while Olivia was sensible and intelligent, she was also wild and impetuous, and it was very, very possible that she'd bitten off far more than she could chew.

Only time, of course, would tell.

THE END

ABOUT THE AUTHOR

Clare Connelly grew up in a small country town in Australia. Surrounded by rainforests, and rickety old timber houses, magic was thick in the air, and stories and storytelling were a huge part of her childhood.

From early on in life, Clare realised her favourite books were romance stories, and read voraciously. Anything from Jane Austen to Georgette Heyer, to Mills & Boon and (more recently) 50 Shades, Clare is a romance devotee. She first turned her hand to penning a novel at fifteen (if memory serves, it was something about a glamorous fashion model who fell foul of a high-end designer. Sparks flew, clothes flew faster, and love was born.)

Clare has a small family and a bungalow near the sea. When she isn't chasing after energetic little toddlers, or wiping fingerprints off furniture, she's writing, thinking about writing, or wishing she were writing.

Clare loves connecting with her readers. Head to **www.clareconnelly.co.uk** to sign up to her newsletter, or join her official facebook page.

BOOKS BY CLARE CONNELLY
SINGLE TITLES
Marrying Her Enemy
The Velasco Lovechild
The Sultan's Reluctant Princess
The Sultan's Virgin Bride
The Sheikh's Arranged Marriage
In the Hands of the Sheikh
One Night with the Sheikh
The Sheikh's Virgin Hostage
To the Highest Bidder
The Greek Tycoon's Forbidden Affair
Bought by the Sheikh
The Billionaire's Christmas Revenge
Tempted by the Billionaire
The Tycoon's Christmas Captive
His Loving Deception
A Second Chance at Love
The Sheikh's Christmas Mistress
Love in the Fast Lane
The Medici Mistress
The Tycoon's Virgin Mistress
All She Wants for Christmas
The Italian Billionaire's Betrayal
A Bed of Broken Promises
Raising the Soldier's Son
The Italian's Innocent Bride
Bartered to the Sheikh
Betrayed by the CEO
COMPENDIUMS
Casacelli Brides
Mediterranean Tycoons
Desert Rulers
Billionaire Bad Boys
Desert Kings

25711885R00094

Printed in Poland
by Amazon Fulfillment
Poland Sp. z o.o., Wrocław